infinity plus

SMOKE PAPER MIRRORS

a short saga for our times

ANNA TAMBOUR

WARNING

This is a work of fiction and fact (all true stuff being certifiably 120 proof). Names, characters, places and incidents, including those in the future, either are products of the author's imagination, or not. Any resemblance to actual events or locales or beings or persons, living or dead or in other states of being, is entirely coincidental, or not. If that gets your knickers in a knot but you wish to proceed, remove knickers now.

Published by infinity plus
www.infinityplus.co.uk
Follow @ipebooks on Twitter

ISBN-13: 978-0-9957522-1-4
ISBN-10: 0995752214

to the S. family

"Assurbanipal, the maniac collector of texts, came just in time. The great culture of his land was already on its way to break up into collector's items."
—Guido Majno, *The Healing Hand: Man and Wound in the Ancient World*, Harvard University Press, 1975 [nabbed for $2 in 2016, w dstjackt, pgs slightly foxed]

[In a shop with a rolling sea of floor and sagging-hammock shelves—in deepest western Sydney—a woman motions to the closed back door.] "There."

[me, pointing to the small range of the best pastries/cookies I've ever eaten anywhere, most of which I've piggily just bought to take away] "*You* made these?"

"Yes." *[embarrassed]*

"Can I tell anyone?"

"... I guess so."

I take pictures of her productions whose perfumes mix with other intoxicants in the dusty air, and lift the camera tentatively.

[she smiles, but shakes her head] "No show me."

"Can I tell your name?"

"Please, no name."

IT COULD BE ARGUED...

...THAT ESCAPEE VANESSA KERSHAWI acted *in flagrante delicto* under the influence, but that is *such* an understatement. There were so many glorious influences, starting with heady freedom.

Within a few waves of her wings, she discovered drink—nectars she'd never known existed, each as intoxicating to suck as it was to see—translucent jellied moats surrounding saffroned puddings, golden falls of lemoned honey oozing from the baklava, the sparkling ice-cold shock of minted rosewatered lemonade, the bittersweet mud of thrice-boiled coffee. The easily liquidized, almost-too-sweet innards of—of *bottled slugs?* She'd never thought to taste a slug's slime. Irresistible, though they made her proboscis curl at their metallic astringency. Her suction tube then stretched out straight to suck the most with the least hindrance of *this perfume-that-you-drink* around the gorgeously complexioned quince...

Drink, rest, drink, rest. She had trouble enough balancing, resting in the open air, when the first curl of hookah smoke reached her. She fanned to catch its drift. Wherever the smoke touched her, it left an invisible mark—a sting of burning sweetness. She perched, stupefied by bliss, as the flavoured wisps snagged, dropping on her one thin veil after another, causing a distinctly unhealthy buzz—*Elma, Kuşüzümü, Misk otu, Gül*—apple, currant, musk plant, rose—and then the one that made her think *Where* have *I* been *all my life?*—*Bubble Gum*. She'd never known this pleasure/pain. Just that morning, before her escape, she'd only known the highest quality care.

And then she was hungry for *it*, a something else, not that she knew what it was, but she wanted it, bad.

And it wasn't as if she snapped her wings and *kazaam*, *it* appeared. She didn't snap her wings.

There were no introductions, no faux chases, no checking each other out, though she must have trailed a reek.

Tail to tail they danced, mutually intoxicated—rolling and twisting, beautifully flailing, tearing scented veils.

If smoke got in their eyes, they didn't blink.

SHE WOULD HAVE BEEN a sight, anyway—as you would expect of anyone called Painted Lady. But seeing her in the act—*them* in it—people's jaws stopped moving or they gobbled "Look!", "Amazing", "Fucken awesome", and grabbed their phones.

"She's so gorgeous," sighed a woman of a certain age, her lips bristling with shards of *börek* pastry. "And what a squirt he is. *So* nothing to look at."

Her sharply-suited companion's thumbs paused their texting. "They're just like birds, Mum. That little nothing's the female."

At that, one of two loiterers standing near nudged the other. They were watching but not impeding anyone's view of the unmistakable sex scene above the hookah corner at Ali Baba's pavement tables.

Indeed, these two men weren't eating, drinking or sharing a water-pipe. They were trying hard to be inconspicuous, but the one who looked like a huge bear with a walrus moustache couldn't still the swaying of his shoulders, hips, and by their side, the sinuous rolling of his wrists, lured by the slow roll of the butterflies. Or possibly both he and the butterflies were entranced by the chastely erotic music mix matched so perfectly to the scene... or the smoke-wreathed act, to it? Does one thing lead to another, and if so, which comes first? What leads if they just go round and round?

"Do butterflies have ears?" wondered the woman who had reached that uncelebrated age called 'certain' as a euphemism for 'invisible', perhaps the kindest cut. She closed her eyes, imagining herself as the dancer, her own slow-smouldering moves... There was time enough in life to unveil her eyes (the horror of a suburban belly-dancing class—all the grace and flexibility of a mob of sheep developing rictus).

A sharp bark of laughter, two appreciative hoots— and a shuffle as the bearlike loiterer lunged at a table.

But it was too late.

At a table of three young men drinking Cokes and sharing a hookah, one guy had got a chokehold on the sinuous neck of the pipe, and swung its head at the mating couple. The terrified butterflies jerked apart and away, presumably as fast as each one could. Vanessa kershawi, the Painted Lady, fled in unsightly saggy loops. Her consort, little Pieris rapae, the Cabbage White, who could have played the part with no need to costume, of one of those scraps of paper always to be found soaked to the floor of a stall at a public toilet—he left the most important scene of his life (an Act he never could have practiced for—a role it was simply outrageous to give him)—he exited with such little (though some would say 'understated') style, no one noticed.

The water-pipe would have burbled again at that table as the pipe was passed if the moustachioed giant, Mr Bülent Bulgurluoğlu, the owner of Ali Baba, hadn't torn the lout out of his chair.

"I've got this, Dad." A younger version of Bulgurluoğlu appeared as if from nowhere, smoothly slipping in.

"Gentlemen." He motioned the men away from Ali Baba's, far enough down the block to frustrate the spectators.

He turned to the three, punching his fists together in front of his face. "Hayden, man. What the!"

"Sami, good you got there. I didn't wanna havta…" The butterfly swatter air-punched a left-right, grinning.

"Actually," Sami Bulgurluoğlu's voice was as professionally smooth and service-industry feminised as when he'd said, 'Gentlemen'. "I had to rescue *you*."

He looked back toward where his father had been, but couldn't… Okay, *there*, just by the tables. The big bear was bent over, examining the base of that syphilitic little excuse for a street tree, as if he'd lost his keys—he and his fellow loiterer, a weedy Chinese guy whose outfit was so colourless and shapeless, he had style.

Sami was tall and hefty as Bulgurluoğlu senior, with a crucial difference. The same massive head, but Sami's bulges were not at his stomach and waist. Muscles burst out of his chest, shoulders and arms and legs.

That idiot laugh again, and a titter. Sami snapped his head around.

"Hay, fuckhead, you're an ass act. And you know? The lot a yuz wasn't funny in school. And youze a fucken sight more unfunny now."

He hadn't raised his voice but he'd stripped it bare.

Hayden pulled his chin in. "Keep your pants on," he said, backing away a step. "How would *I* know your old man's into moth porn?"

One of the chorus boys who'd grown a little happyface smile, put a hand up. "Yeah, our bad, man. Keep it cool." He was holding his mobile in front of him like a shield.

Cowards, the three of them—but opportunists. Sami Bulgurluoğlu's gut twisted with fear—*Mom, Dad, Hurrem, Ali Baba's.*

"I'm just into butterflies," he said, putting on a falsetto and making himself slouch. "But seriously, guys. Ali Baba's not your scene, geddit? See you at the gym tomorrow, assholes."

They swaggered away, but not before everyone watching saw one of the chorus boys reach out and give their leader's head a swat. Sami had turned back already, so he didn't see nor hear "You *are* a fuckhead, y'know. That butterfly shit was cool."

THAT BUTTERFLY SHIT. LIKE all shit, there was a before and after, and a *before* before—and an *after* after—and an infinity to drive you nuts, of *later*s.

One such:

"A line is just something unfinished for it has an end. 'Glorious' is a poisoned clot dumped upon a line to stunt its growth. Wipe away the clot and the line can grow—and every line that can grow all the way, grows into a circle that never ends."

Mr Bulgurluoğlu could hardly believe that his friend, who'd been obsessed for months, was talking such. . . such *waffle*.

So before getting back to the butterflies and what they did *after*, let's ignore the circle and pick a point—somewhere along Mr Bulgurluoğlu's friend's *before*.

MR ZHANG'S MATERNAL great-grandfather Jin Youwei could have been an insect, so often did he shed his skin and take on a new persona. He had to, having risen quickly in the Qing civil service from mere interpreter (fourth class) in the Chinese Embassy at Paris, to interpreter (third class) in Berlin, second class in London, and in a 'disgracefully short time' said the envious, to the Moscow post of Ambassador to the Court of Tsar Nicolas II, where he was instrumental in the 1896 treaty between the Qing and Tsarist empires that gave the Russians the right to run the Trans-Siberian railroad from Manchuria to Vladivostok while guaranteeing China territorial integrity. The Russians also agreed to pay China's otherwise ruinous and disgraceful debt to imperialist Japan imposed as the result of a treaty that diplomat Jin Youwei had nothing to do with, he made sure everyone knew—a treaty so fresh, it was still wet with humiliation.

Flitting from city to city, language to language, uppercrust Mandarin to provincial peasant's slang, Ambassador Jin could have been a butterfly, he travelled so much. But immediately after that treaty came a period where he was stuck in Beijing, weighed down by promotion upon promotion. Minister of the Office of Foreign Affairs, and on top of that, Minister of this, and that. Any normal man would have been smothered in this growing pile of downy quilts, but not his Honourable snug self.

He acted like the ancient hypochondriac Chu Xilien, who wouldn't get out of bed no matter what the danger. When the Yellow River rampaged across the land, drowning landlord and peasant alike, it tore through his house and picked him up as if the waters were looking just for him. The river deposited him neatly on a mountain he'd always wished to visit before it receded to its own usual bed. Chu Xilien had many bedly adventures and he was provisioned for every contingency. Medicine, of course. And food and drink and rockets, so all he had to do when he wanted portage was to fire off a rocket or two.

Chu Xilien's smoke-dragons were famous. The mere smell of one would bring you luck, and if you were part of the portage party, your grandchildren's lives would be legendarily fortunate. Yet all the tales of Chu Xilien added up to a slim volume. The Ambassador (Jin Youwei liked that simple title best) was a modern Chu Xilien with a much bigger tome in construction.

While the fiercest of winds took the world by the throat, shaking the blood from its broken neck, he was calm as a well-fed baby—and airborne, deep in his bed of many covers, floating peacefully in the cold quiet eye of the hurricane. When a suffocatingly thick cover dropped atop the rest—the Grand Secretariat and Attendant Gentleman of the Ministry of Rites— he didn't even sweat, though maybe the next cover was too much. Or maybe it was a touch of wind.

He successfully burrowed under his pile during the Palace coup that resulted in the young reformist (one person's reformist is another's collaborationist) emperor being put under house arrest in the Forbidden City—his advisors known as the Six Gentlemen being treated to death while others fled. None of them had advocated expelling foreign devils. All of them had wanted to get rid of the lazy careerists in the civil service, the ones who had worked the system for years. The new ruler of the Empire was the highly effective manipulator Empress Dowager Cixi, as supremely confident in her dislike of foreigners and their pernicious influences as she was in her disdain of change. Jin Youwei, the polyglot cosmopolitan diplomat, watched in dismay but wisely acted as the hypochondriac, as he not only valued his head, but more than that, his Precious.

Sometimes in his exalted positions, how he envied the lowly—the high cannot hide in bed forever. He had to get out but was faced with the eternal problem: *Which side?*

A moment past the coup that tried to turn back history, the Boxer Rebellion blew up in blood. In his position as Minister of Education, he administered from his virtual bed, but it didn't protect him. He caught a fever that made him throw off the covers and meet with others such as the Vice-President of the Court of Sacrifices. There was no time to waste. He banished the Chu Xilien metaphor to his own history where they both might meet again, and put on a hypermodern metaphoric coat fit for this new century.

For the first time in his life, he had to take unwonted action, first and decisively, *now* (meaning 'within hours', an alien concept to a diplomat). He had no choice. *To survive a gale, be in front of it.*

The Boxer Rebellion was stirring up a hurricane of spattered foreign-devil blood. Blood that *would* be avenged, with usurious interest.

The Society of the Righteous and Harmonious Fists, which foreigners called the Boxers—was a popular secret movement of poverty-stricken young men with no opportunities: discharged soldiers, landless peasants; craftsmen, tradesmen, tinkers put out of livelihood. And astounding as it might seem, out-of-work black-marketeers.

They protected themselves with exercises for the mind and spirit that made them impervious to bullets, so it was said. They were, above all, traditionalists, so of course women could not join their ranks. But women did form their own patriotic units. The powers of the Red Lanterns were said to exceed those of the brave men they were helping. These women could not only walk on water, but fly. And bullets? They could stop them with a look. And they excelled at the sneak attack, burning down a church while being seen dutifully hoeing a field a mountainside away.

To the convenience of the Empress Dowager Cixi, Fists and Lanterns alike blamed everything on the foreign devils.

Christian missionaries spread perversion and disrespect of gods and ancestors as they stole land to plant their temples on. Worst of all, they had finagled a right to do this, imposed by treaty. It all was part of a foreign conspiracy, a diabolical plot not just to corrupt the minds of the people, but to starve their bodies. Western powers were putting millions out of work by dumping cheap foreign-made imports, as they carved up China and served it to themselves like the ghosts who ate the Christmas repast. British, Americans, Germans, Russians, Japanese, Austro-Hungarians, *even the Italians who stole our noodle technology and called it theirs*—all alike and on the take, force-feeding China this unfair trade.

At first the patriots hit easy targets in the countryside. Small stuff, but their successes gave them confidence. The Empress Dowager Cixi was said to 'dither' but how could that be? She was delighted. So was the whole dynastic family. Prince Duan himself had become the effective leader of this lot of disaffected masses, fighting for her and hers.

She ordered Qing Imperial Forces to help, but the Qing dynasty under her was hardly a government of national unity, despite the slogan of the Righteous and

Harmonious Fists: *Support Qing government and exterminate the foreigners.*

The foreigners demanded a stop to this nonsense, which only inspired more slogans and added to the legends. *Did you know the Fists can also repel knives?*

On the 10th of June, 1900, at the Battle of Langfang, it wasn't just 'irregulars' but 5,000 troops surprisingly well motivated and supplied, who won a victory against a smug international coalition led by a British Vice-Admiral. That gave them courage to carry on, and soon terrifying rumours spread amongst foreigners even as lines of communication were cut.

In Beijing, German Imperial Envoy, Baron Klemens Freiherr von Ketteler was so incensed at this impunity that against advice, he left the walled foreign legation compound to take his complaint directly to the Palace. On his way, he was slain in his sedan chair. But word of his dispatch was carried back, and that might have been why the residents didn't evacuate as the Palace demanded, but burrowed in.

Two days later, on the 20th of June, the Boxer forces swept into Beijing. Wiping their bloody hands, they paused, laying siege to the Christmas feast itself—the foreign legation compound replete with fat ambassadors, foreign devils, and traitors.

The next morning, the Empress Dowager Cixi gave the besieging force her firm support, helping the common people in every way short of making their lives better.

"The foreigners have been aggressive toward us," said her declaration of war. "The common people suffer greatly at their hands and everyone is vengeful."

Ambassador Jin Youwei was beside himself with foresight.

Empress Dowager Cixi, however, was so proudly ignorant of history and confident in her judgment, her counsel so kowtowing, that he could only address her by petition. Thus, the gist of what he wrote was: *With respect, your most Esteemed and... breaching international law and murdering foreign diplomats is gravely undiplomatic.* She was too sensitive to truth, often reacting violently, so he couldn't expose the whole hideous blood-dripping situation to her. He had to treat her with the utmost delicacy but nevertheless had to give her his undiluted, urgent prognosis: she and the Empire could only hope to survive, with multiple amputations—under no anaesthetic—if they bowed their heads.

"Off with his head," said the Empress, or something like that. Court documents condemn Jin

Youwei for 'wilfully and absurdly petitioning the Imperial Court' and 'building subversive thought'.

On the 23rd of June, his head would surely have been crisping on a spike in Beijing's roasting summer air if he hadn't been the diplomat he was, plus.

IT IS STILL ARGUED what happened. At dawn the morning after his execution was announced, a lady rushed to that famous park in Beijing, the Caishikou Execution Grounds. She had no problem obtaining entry. This was a popular time for the guards to work. She didn't ask directions, for she knew what she was looking for, so she rushed right in.

A few rows down and one turn to the left, she yelled, "Stop here" to her sedan porters. There, still shining with dampness on the spike, was the once-exalted head of Ambassador Minister petitioner subversive Jin Youwei.

A park attendant strolled close at that moment. She had her coins ready.

He counted them, and nodded. *The whole thing. She must be rich.*

He pulled a filthy sack out of his pants, pulled the head off the spike, bagged it, tied it closed and handed it to the woman, who gave him a clean full sack.

He pulled a head out of the clean bag and stuck it on the spike. It looked the twin of the one he'd removed.

"Home," she said as she closed the curtains. "Quick." The summer heat was already almost unbearable. And she couldn't wait to get home with the present.

Home was a 45-minute run away, and in all that time, she didn't complain once about the bumps. Her husband's nameday was tomorrow, and all she could think of was their joy.

By tomorrow night he would be a new man, and promotion would follow promotion, respect would pile upon respect. He would be resented, of course, and envied—but raised up out of danger. Their lives would be as joyful as two dissolute frogs supping from on a lily pad on a lake glittering with insects. No more would he be a bottom-level translator bringing home stories about the exploits and talents of the exalted.

She'd scrimped and saved the household money. She'd fed him only cheap sorghum buns and pickled turnips and herself just pickled vegetables for months, to get a chance to get just one dose, one scrap of flesh. That he hadn't complained made her all the more determined. He'd just quietly read some silly French books to dream away his life because the powerless have no way else to rise. Meanwhile, she never rested. She pounced on every rumour, never missed a death notice, stayed ever vigilant, making her detailed plan. Finally, she had saved enough for a scrap, but no one would do.

No one, no one, till last night. Her husband came home late, pale as a candle and reeking of hard strong *baijiu*.

"We're all doomed," he said, the scrap of paper falling from his hand.

That famous face, and the announcement. *Jin Youwei's execution!* The man her husband hated, he loved so much, had wanted so much to *be*.

She undressed her insensate husband and put him to bed, gathered up a bundle and in blessed darkness, ran to a hock shop where she had planned to bang on the door to have the owner open up, but where it on the contrary, was busier than ever. There she traded in all the jewellery passed down to her and everything else she could carry of worth, including her husband's fob watch. Especially that. It was a hand-me-down from Jin Youwei. Her husband only wore it on special occasions and didn't trust himself to wind the thing.

Then she went to a certain unmarked door and up some stairs, where she paid most of her money. The next morning at dawn she went up those stairs again, picked up her purchase, and in a nearby park, hired the sedan chair because she supposed only semi-powerful women could do this kind of thing.

Speeding to that special park, the Caishikou Execution Grounds, she made her transaction as she had heard one does, if one is semi-powerful enough.

Mind you, this cure isn't one that just anyone can avail oneself of. The recipe for success can only be used by those successful enough to rise from an already risen position. She was really too low, thus the need to scrimp and hock. But she loved her husband and knew he needed special help.

The recipe goes thus: *If dry, crush and powder. If still wet, flay, cut, or chop. Add to boiling water. All the powers transfer themselves to the drinker, plus one that the original owner of the head never had. Invincibility.* She'd heard some say *Immortality*, but she wasn't greedy, nor gullible. Jin Youwei's original powers and talents, his extraordinary level of success and respect, minus his downfall. That was enough for her. She couldn't wait to dose her husband.

"Stop here," she ordered the sedan porters still far from her home, not wanting them to know she lived in such a poor area.

Home she scurried, the filthy bag secured under her robes. The thing surprised her. She had expected to be rather repulsed by this extravagant medicine, the *whole head*, at that. But of the odours rising up from her sweaty chest, she could only smell sweet success.

She made herself wait till her husband came home, and then flipped the bag open at his feet.

The head hit dully on the bare wood floor, and rocked to a standstill under their horrified eyes.

Wax! It could have been a copy of the wax one she had paid for.

"Someone else must have got there first," she said dully.

"Maupassant," he mumbled, quite a nonsense answer, so he must have been talking to himself.

Oh, well, he consoled himself, knowing that this was what all her secret planning had led up to. There wasn't a damn thing he could have done to stop her. She was so young, yet so old-fashioned in some ways, believing ridiculous, gruesome superstition. But she was in other ways, quite modern. She genuinely loved him. And she sacrificed more. He didn't need to look to know she had no jewellery now, so he couldn't be too heartbroken about the loss of his watch, *given to me by the great man himself one day when he saw I was reading something he called 'worthwhile'.*

He tried hard to feel romantic about her sacrifice, but he couldn't help resenting her. *That precious watch!* It hadn't worked, granted, needing a British watchmaker. *But nothing can replace it.*

If only he were shallow—one can read too much into things. She hadn't sold the watch. She'd only pawned it. If he'd only told her of his grief, they could have redeemed the silly sentimental thing the next day. Instead, he assumed she'd sold it, held that against her in a bitter corner of his heart till the day he died, and some other man with aspirations got the watch six months after his wife hocked it. The new owner never made it work but never got rid of it, so this item with *London* emblazoned on its face became the key player in another story of a type the reader of worthwhiles never read, for why would he want to relax with twisted horror?

But that was the future. Back to his present.

"Dry your tears," he said. "Let's get some pork dumplings. And thank you for this beautiful memento." He smoothed out the dent in the wax cheek and stuck the head deep in his bookcase, safely peeking from the shadows. He could never tell his wife, but she'd given him a present he could never have hoped for. From being doomed to be a lowly public servant for life, she turned him into a romantic literary figure. *Who, in this life, can ask for more?*

The flesh-and-blood head was safely attached and far away, having planned far better than the lowest-level-interpreter's wife.

Beijing's July and August are hellishly hot to take in the outdoor sights, so it was only in October, before bitter cold set in, that the tourism business usually thrived and the pleasures of the Caishikou Execution Grounds were sought out by the throng. However, this year was exceptional. So much was happening that visits for that other purpose were increasing daily. Many a purposeful lady was incensed, some desperate, to find that she'd arrived too late to obtain her first or second choice. Only a reform thought up by the lowliest staff member on the last day of June saved the day for the staff as a whole— not just their gratuities but *maybe our heads?* A sign was made and hung outside the gates. In big characters: *Come at 11 am daily for the freshest of heads!*

AMBASSADOR JIN YOUWEI HAD managed to keep his head above politics, having escaped only two years previously being a party to the Hundred Days Reform movement. While he privately considered the reforms utterly necessary for the survival of the Qing dynasty, he judged the movement: utterly doomed. The Empress Dowager Cixi was a much craftier player than the starry-eyed movement actors. She topped them and he floated up with her when the fighting cooled, like so much congealed fat. But he'd always known that one day he would put a foot wrong, so he hadn't really expected the ignorant, stubborn woman to want to see the world as it is.

He despised those who cared nothing for preparing, so he, therefore, had put everything in place *before* he sent his petition, and was already safe when the Empress Dowager erupted.

His philosophy as a career public servant had always been *Don't ask. Don't refuse* bribes. This had made him extremely financially independent, with great wealth spread discreetly around the world.

He had three great loves: theatre, tea, and his daughter. Well, maybe four: reading. No. It must be The Five Treasures: Daughter (his Precious), Reading, Books, Theatre, Tea. The many languages he'd mastered were the keys that dangled from his neck, ever ready.

He never bothered with loving anything unless he was willing to *jump into the sea and learn to swim*. In the Sea of Theatre, he became a master of disguise, costume, dummy-making, sculpture, and rôle-playing. The Sea of Reading almost drowned him when a hefty gestalt hit him. He'd collected, in the Sea of Books, a floating *city* of books, none of which he could abandon, especially his precious immortal *Quan Tangshi* (Complete Collection of Tang Poems) still going strong almost two centuries after its publication. He lived another life when he picked up this unwieldy clattering bundle, becoming Li Bao, that lover of life, wine, beautiful women and nature, embracer of necessary sadness and loss. The poet's only fault was his pampering of nostalgia, which the seasoned statesman considered baggage that could weigh a person down, fatally. The other book he treasured was his signed copy of Gogol's *Dead Souls*.

This floating city of books was a constant problem. It took up innumerable travelling cases and much space wherever Jin went, even though he had, employing his theatre-set skills, ingeniously designed and carpentered the cases to unfold into instant library shelves. He was ashamed to admit to himself that once he made this portable library, the cases/shelves themselves added to the worry. He got a pain in his chest at the thought of somehow losing the books and the cases, having to give them away—till the great man himself, Li Bao, arrived unannounced one night in a dream.

The poet was too refined to express his true disgust, but he smelt like camphor and burnt moustache ends—and they *were* frizzled.

"What you harbour," he said, sitting himself on the mat, "is a housekeeper's emotion. And you stand there without offering me tea?"

In the dream the Ambassador looked frantically for tea but the only tea to be found was a ball the size of a pumpkin clutched in the pages of a book which was seated on a horse, speeding away toward the Point of Infinity. Frustratingly, the horses' hooves were distinct as the tapping fingernails of an impatient emperor. The book's pages shook with laughter. With the certain knowledge only dreams possess, Jin knew that the book was the precious immortal *Quan Tangshi* that held all of Li Bao's poems.

"Good riddance," said the ancient poet. "Tip that book all you like. No tea will come from it. And now to you. If you truly love us, read what we have to say. Remember it, and be free."

Jin Youwei bowed, stunned by this generous imparting of knowledge that would free his life.

"Wine!" ordered the poet.

"At once," answered his acolyte.

Luckily for him, wine appeared before both of them, filling their cups without needing to be lifted to the task.

"Remembering is swimming without needing to move your limbs," Li Bao said, licking his cup. "Or swimming is remembering. Aren't you going to get that book?"

They were both pretty sozzled by then. Jin Youwei wobbled as he ran with the little old poet on his back. It was such a long way to the Point of Infinity, but he made it.

"I'll get off here," said Li Bao. The horse wasn't so accommodating. Jin Youwei had to carry the huge volume all the way home, but this time the shore of the sea tossed him a wave, and he rode it all the way to the Sea of Books.

Luckily for the ambassador, he was in the habit of remembering his dreams, so when he woke, he had no doubts what his future path should be.

He still swam daily in the Sea of Reading and the Sea of Books, but he no longer needed to keep the floating city of books. He only needed to read something once to add it permanently to his between-the-ears library, which kept getting bigger all the time though it took up no more space.

To get to his daughter, we need first, to swim past the Straits of his Wife.

She was a traditional Chinese woman, raised to serve her husband and be obedient and silent in his and his father's presence. Highly decorative, she might have been as frustrated as the wives of Parisian, English, and Russian diplomats looked to him. He didn't know. What he did know was that he and his wife had nothing in common other than their class. She could play several instruments very well, and she directed the servants well enough that there weren't always new ones. But she could not be taken abroad—insisting to wear what would be seen as her ridiculously old-fashioned and impractical dress. She could no more learn to wear a corset than she could unbind her lotus feet.

Their four sons were her joy, and they were typical for their class. He sometimes wondered what would happen to them in the changing world, but they were so self-satisfied and dull that he couldn't bring himself to care. His daughter, on the other hand, that great disappointment to her mother because she was not the auspicious bringer of good fortune, the fifth boy, made the aging diplomat wish he were a poet. He knew for the first time in his life, the meaning of *love at first sight*. Indeed, the love he tried to hide was so obvious to his wife that within a week, the baby's unseeing eyes were huge from starvation. He didn't know babies, but guessed. He'd only been at home that week because of her, so when he left with her, his going was hardly remarked upon, and her being gone wasn't noticed for days.

Her brothers and mother were happy to be rid of Little Shame who they assumed had been given away or something more extreme but much better for the future. None of them missed the master of the house.

It all ran so much better without him so long as he kept funding the household, not that his money was needed. Her family was more wealthy, but did want this marriage for his international prestige.

The baby (her father named her Jin Libao) was an impractical companion, but from Paris to Berlin, London to Moscow, diplomats and their wives, servants and masters, little old ladies and pet dogs— everyone was charmed. She teethed on a set of language keys, and soon her head was filling with a growing library. She was clearly a child prodigy, but that wasn't what really did the trick of fascinating all. The looks between father and daughter brought many a pragmatic, cynical soul to the brink of joy.

JIN LIBAO WAS ALREADY seven years old when her father sent that petition to the Dowager Empress. Travelling with Father was always so exciting for her, especially when they were other people. This trip started out as the most thrilling so far, for she knew where his head was supposed to be.

They were some of the first brave souls to take the Trans-Siberian train from Irkutsk to Moscow, where the ambassador had many dear, discreet old friends. Father and daughter were special guests in fancifully carved country dachas where they were fed as if they weren't stateless wanderers, as if starving peasants weren't close enough to sniff the kitchen's fumes: *blinis* thick as quilts, smothered with sour cream and wild strawberries in rosy syrup; the giant pie known as *koulebiaka* built as sturdy as the Forbidden City, and like it, filled with treasures—salmon as firm as if it were still leaping, forest mushrooms smelling headily of rain and recent death, pheasant eggs, the gland of a fish that is said to be a myth. . . and vodka colder than ice, for vodka can never freeze.

All this, and swansdown-filled mattresses were offered to these special guests. Father and daughter were perfectly charming, even though it was a tragedy that by the second day of their stay, no matter the dacha, he asked for them to only be served with the simplest *grechnevaya kasha* buckwheat groats, *and water if you please.*

On the road, they ate much worse. In China, mouldy buckwheat porridge, years' old rice cakes marbled yellow and green as the peasants ate them if there were any left to dig up when the harvest failed or was burned or stolen or taken in tax. Father taught daughter how to filter muddy water from puddles, and how to keep it in you when you cannot filter but must lie down and suck it with a muddy face. He had, from her earliest days, tried to prepare her for adventure, for danger, for cheating those who would introduce her to Death.

ON THIS TRIP, THEY flitted from country house to country estate of members of the Court of Nicolas II, until the writing was on the wall, but they didn't flee. They waited till change was being writ in blood—and suddenly, it seemed to the unobservant, they were on a ship bound for San Francisco where they both learned what 'Chinese food' tastes like.

They started off in sophisticated San Francisco as Mr and Mrs Arkhem Wu, she being a very small and lithe ten years old, lovely and fragile as a mayfly— enchantingly pure. Their first need was to get the folding green stuff, which they achieved from a meeting with a collector of rare miniature pictures of a certain athletic type. Faux husband and wife dined on mock turtle soup, turkey with oyster stuffing and slabs of apple pie heavy as gold bullion while their host salivated over their private times. His imagination led him to pay an insanely thick wad for the kind of fifth-rate porn created and sold to poor missionaries and Jesuit priests from Shanghai to Denpassar.

After San Francisco, Jin Youwei took his daughter to sea again, up the coast to Astoria, a bustling fish and timber port.

Their destination would be evident as the first sight of Astoria, he'd been told. Jin Youwei's eyes crinkled when it loomed out from the fog. Believing the stories of natural bullshitters takes skill.

Mother Hoolihan's—Bed like Mother would make & the Biggest Drinks from Santiago to Nome. The sign was huge. The balcony was as romantic as a seaman's carved loving spoon. and you needn't walk into the dump of a town that stunk of salmon canneries. Mother Hoolihan's sprawled out on its own pier.

The seamen's dormitory was upstairs. Its lovely *Wherefore art thou* balcony jutted out over the water, all ironwork curlicued just as he'd been told. A ship owner told him its secret. Under the rose-patterned oilcloth carpet was a trapdoor chute that worked so sweetly that Mother's boys could load a ship's tender with an order of men she'd successfully mickied easy as a timber-merchant delivering a cord of wood. The need for ships' crews was so great and so competitive, that without the transfer of insensate men up to the waiting vessels, the port would have been becalmed. On waking, a seaman was so hung over, he'd be too sick to complain till land was but a bitter memory.

A seaman only gets paid if he makes the return journey on the same ship. Also, there are ships and trips no seaman wants to go on, so shanghaiing eliminated the supply problems captains would otherwise have had while supplying owners of all ships in this system free workers if seamen somehow missed their boat and were loaded onto another. Boarding house masters were encouraged to slip those mickies by being given a bounty for every seaman. And Mrs Hoolihan had the distinction of being the most favoured seamen's stop in the West, by ship owners and seamen alike. Men knew she was dangerous, but her drinks were the biggest, her beds so soft and clean, and her grub like a loving mother's. You just had to remember to be careful. That was what Jin Youwei had been told.

They entered the bar. It was obvious who Mother Hoolihan was. She could elegantly-as-you-please toss a buffalo with even her left (more delicate than right) pinkie. She bustled over, wiping her hands on a surprisingly clean apron. He bowed, straightened up, and clicked his heels.

"Well, I do," she said, and something made her hold out her hand, the colour and firmness of skinned salmon.

He took it in one gloved hand, and raised it near his lips. She could feel his breath before he released her.

"Mrs Hoolihan, I have heard such good things about you," he said. "I am Arthur Chin and this is my daughter Lily."

His daughter stepped forward next to him and stuck out her hand, shaking Mrs Hoolihan's American-businessman style.

"Drop me dead widout me dinner," said Mother Hoolihan.

"Pleased ta meet ya," said the girl with such confidence that Myra Hoolihan, all three hundred pounds of muscle, roared. She believed in family, so would have fed these two, who tickled her, the best she had, what she served herself and her sons. Great bloody steaks the size of shipping maps, a Mt St Helens of mashed spuds, cherry cobbler as slickly red and white as the heads of so many shanghaied 'sailors', escapees from the seas of grain who don't learn how to hold onto a clewline fast enough.

"We're not your usual hotel," said Mother Hoolihan, blushing.

"Delighted," said Mr Chin.

He had sought her out for a purpose that he explained, once they withdrew to her parlour. He wanted her to educate his daughter. And thus, Mrs Hoolihan became a private governess of sorts.

The Hoolihan family's special poison, the best or worst in the world, depending upon your point of view, was fed to the girl as if it were malted milk. This was the wish of not just her father, which horribly enough, was a request Mrs Hoolihan was used to but had never previously fulfilled. No, this child *demanded* it. "To toughen me up," she said. "So that no one can put anything over on me."

If the Hoolihan mother and sons had been dogs, they would have rolled over for this girl. The biggest hulk, Pericles Hoolihan, actually lost his appetite when Lily said to her father one night at dinner while choking down a steak, "I reckon I'm done here, Pops."

When they left, Mrs Hoolihan stoically smiled and waved beside her red-faced sons who were mopping their own faces as if they were dandies, but in bed she soaked her pillow and sounded like a geriatric bulldog. Captain Hoolihan had never lit her gizzard like this Chinaman did. Far from being some Yellow Peril beast, he made her dream that she was a learned lady, able to take his hand and stroll the world. And his daughter! What a beauty she would be.

JIN YOUWEI HAD NEVER known till sending that petition how attracted he was to danger. How he didn't want to live in safety and ignorance. How much he hated being coddled in an out-of-the-way country house. Far more thrilling it would be to run from a burning Summer Palace. Of course this was out of the question with a daughter, especially this extraordinary treasure.

Bah to that! said his daughter, who it turned out by the time they reached this strange 'United States', was even worse. Every outraged look she received as a beautiful young chink in this country where the Chinese Exclusion laws required all Chinese living in the United States to register or face deportation— each look made her want to compare her supposedly yellow skin with that roast-rooster skin of the Americans; want to make her eyes, black and shapely as a printer's swash, a point size smaller and more slitty. Every outfit she wore, from the most in-the-mode evening gown worn to the New York Metropolitan Opera, to the most modest navy serge suit matching the tambourine bangers on Meany Street—everything she wore when the two of them weren't in obvious side-show costume, was *wrong, if you ask me*, as sniffy onlookers loved to state without being asked. Funny, that.

From the sidelong and backward glances and outright stares, plenty of men travelling rough, smooth, and riding roughshod on life, didn't give a damn what she wore. That face, that grace, that individualism, that voice that was so intimidating for if you were forward enough to say anything to her, some little pleasantry or a boast, she was all politeness and smiles, answering you right back *but in your voice*. Then she'd likely turn to her father? husband? owner? who could tell?—and talk like the three drunk crows who meet in a 'Frisco bar, one from Transylvania, one from Chile, and one who hatched in the eaves of that bar on Market Street, but who was so drunk he couldn't understand a word he was saying. Now, where was that story going? *That girl is confusing!*

No wonder! She and her father had a game they kept expanding. Stuff as many languages and dialects in a sentence as possible, trying to trip the other up. They called the game *Bamboozle*. He had thought American 'English' would be too crude to have fun with, but as with all languages, it had treasures that could not be imitated, especially the evangelising dialects out for your wallet, your soul.

Whatever father and daughter spoke to each other—from temple-bird-music of nine-tone street-vendor Cantonese to the whetstone scrape of top-level Beijing Mandarin, to the hopeless romanticism of Russian, the self-confidence of French, the gloriously diseased Czech—riven with consonants— daughter and father played Bamboozle so constantly and so fast, it was a wonder they didn't confuse themselves. No one else had a hope.

They roamed widely, he making sure they ate the most inedible garbage available. In Sydney, the worst meat pies in the world—dry crusts encasing hairballs in gravy. In Chile, a silly mistake that proved a lesson. Never confuse *higado* with *pescado*, for if *higado* (liver) is white as fish and has what looks like very small print on it, the most toughened constitution will revolt.

They flitted, soaking up experiences, skirting danger, acting out fantasies with ever-new disguises.

Years passed filled with international spite, anger, viciousness and intrigue.

Jin Libao thoroughly enjoyed being the sinister Chinese magician's Mongolian Monkeybear—a ridiculous costume that everyone in Podunk believed the gospel truth. Hell, that was fun!

They were the best of travelling companions/conspirators, fellow moths drawn to the flame.

Yokohama. They arrived in the dark. Early the next morning they left their inn a block from the harbour to see the sights. They were a sight, too: Toshihiro Kiyonobu, a famous detective from Tokyo, and his assistant Kawanabe, whose dapper moustache was making its wearer itch. This was their most daring set of disguises yet. And the most fun. Jin Libao's was even more of a triumph than her father's. She was already eighteen years old, her cheeks were naturally the texture and hue of the most delicate rubbed spring peach, and her gait when not disguised flowed like a stream—not this quick, choppy, acolytic servility.

The two of them had no plans for the day as such, though it being a fishing port, they did hope to catch some looks.

They hadn't gone a hundred steps when a man ran out of a bookstall and approached them, stuttering. He held a book out and opened his mouth to speak, but was stricken with a bowing fit. Kawanabe handed the detective a pen. The great Toshihiro Kiyonobu signed the book and presented it to the man by holding it on both of his hands, saying, "It is never too late," words that the poor bookseller spent the rest of his life trying to crack.

The famous detective, assistant in tow, rushed purposefully to the harbour.

Mist was rising from the sea, swirling playfully around the lovely swollen bellies of home-hugging fishing boats, slipping down like stowaway ghosts into holds of unromantic business-built barques loading to cross the seas.

In character, he gesticulated, pointed out things, stroked his chin and talked, his assistant devotedly scribbling notes.

"A good likeness of me, don't you think?" he said, jutting his chin out at the biggest ship.

She turned up her lip, forgetting how moustache hairs up the nose feel like a loving miniature hedgehog. "That cover didn't do you justice. You should have been painted by Kawanabe Kyosai. Too bad he's dead."

"As if that's any impediment," her father said tartly.

"Now don't go cryptic on me, you ol—"

She fell hard, bashing her knee.

Behind her, she heard gurgling, choking, the sickening sound of a head being bashed against stones.

She rolled over and kicked up, striking air. Her father's assailant laughed, hitting out with his left fist while his right got in another punch. "Got *you!*" he growled. "You'll never catch *me.*"

Whack! Bash!

"Eh!"

Footsteps. The scream of a whistle. More footsteps, the thud of a thick hemp belaying rope against a human head. Clatters, scrapes.

The obsequious cries and horror of the beat policeman.

The great detective's face was so battered that his assistant immediately wrapped it in a handkerchief.

The assistant's trousers were torn and he would have quite a black eye. Quite rightly, however, he only had thoughts for his master.

"Honourable sir," said the policeman to the detective. "What do you wish me to do with *this*?"

The assailant dangled from his grasp.

The detective nodded at one of the many fishermen who'd gathered.

"You saw this policeman detain this criminal, did you not?"

"With pleasure." The fisherman didn't know what this gentleman's business was on the wharf, but a thug who would beat up an older man of obvious intellect as well as trip his assistant, a man of youth and fitness, is a dastardly deviant—definitely a fish thief.

"Sergeant," said the older man. "You have done the Japanese people a great service in apprehending Nakamura Bentaro."

"The Butterfly!"

"None other."

Toshihiro Kiyonobu had been after this master of escape for his whole celebrated career. Everyone knew it, these two pitted against each other, gambling with death.

"Bentaro had been meaning to escape on the Marie Brassiere there, off to Vancouver, weren't you?"

"Some day," promised the Butterfly, putting so much meaning into his scowl that it's a shame this isn't told with a picture.

THE POLICEMAN WAS SO awed and so overly honest that as he reported the incident, the great detective recognized the criminal, chased him and made the citizen's arrest. Toshihiro Kiyonobu then handed the Butterfly to the only person around who represented the police force: the humble him.

"So where is Kiyonobu?" thundered his chief. "Don't tell me 'I don't know'."

The policeman hung his head.

All day the force looked, but as they expected, the master of disguise had disappeared.

The police chief was heartbroken. His idol. So close...

As for the real great detective, what he thought when he heard of his most famous exploit—the one that finally ended in catching The Butterfly—one can only speculate.

SEAGULLS WHEEL AND CRY in the wake of the *Selkirkshire*, the 1,237 ton iron barque coming into Astoria from Yokohama. Father and daughter are doing something they've not done before. *Mother Hoolihan's—Bed like Mother would make & the Biggest Drinks from Santiago to Nome* comes into view.

Revisiting anywhere is a new experience.

"MRS HOOLIHAN," HE SAID solemnly. A sob burst from her soul. She put out her hand and then threw her arms around him.

"Let them talk," she said.

"Ma!" Pericles burst through the door, his arms full of bags. He was closely followed.

"Lily!" Myra Hoolihan always tried to keep her crying to a minimum, but this was all too much. Her bosom and muscles took up so much space, she hadn't enough air, so the sound was soon answered by the town's most emotional donkey.

"I *never*," she wheezed out. Pericles just watched.

"Mr Chin," she finally said. "You do us proud. And your young lady here. Why, Lily, you are the ticket. I swore you'd grow up to be a flower, but you're the whole bouquet."

"The garden," uttered Pericles.

"The damnblasted forest," said his brother Aloysius, to the unguardedly jealous glance of Pericles. Love had helped him by putting 'the garden' in his mouth, but then why did it turn around and give Al that 'damnblasted forest' gift, which must be much more poetic since it didn't mean a damnblasted thing, far as he could figger.

All that love swirling here, but this visit couldn't be no sentimental saunter.

"You're safe here," said Myra Hoolihan. "Now what is it you need? No. Don't tell us yet. Boys, get to it."

In a half hour, father and daughter were soaking in two enormous tin baths in the two best bedrooms in the Hoolihans' part of the house.

Mrs Hoolihan was cooking up a storm, singing as she beat biscuit dough till it would rise in heavenly blisters, her loud but musical voice calling "I'm only a bird in a gilded cage."

They all got the story at dinner.

Mr Chin and his daughter had travelled for years, as the Hoolihans knew. They had first to escape the evil Empress Dowager Cixi of China, who wanted to put Mr Chin's head on a stick like a candy apple. And then they had to escape other bad people. Mr Chin particularly had to keep his precious daughter from being hurt or stolen by bad people. The world is full of bad people, is it not?

Myra Hoolihan nodded to break her neck, and so did her sons. They all knew their manners and would have died rather than talk now with their mouths open.

Mr Chin looked more distinguished than ever, but tired-like.

He was too polite to refuse food, but Mrs Hoolihan remembered now how eating had always kind of bothered this two. Not seeing her or her sons eat. No. They seemed to enjoy that, encourage that. It hit Myra Hoolihan all of a sudden like a twist in the gut. *They can't afford to give themselves pleasure.*

"Mrs Hoolihan," he said, "I won't be able to protect Lily forever. Would you have some more to teach her?

"And," he butted in before she could answer. "If it doesn't inconvenience you too awfully much, could we rest with you and your wonderful sons a while, and take pleasure in your company?" He had the most genuine, romantic smile she'd ever seen. And it *was* genuine.

"What happened to the Evil Empress?" asked Pericles. He hoped Lily would answer but was too shy to look at her.

"Well!" she said, her tinkling laugh making the canary sound like a chicken being shooed with an umbrella.

"Only a month or two after she would have had my father's head," she said, "the evil old Empress had to escape herself. We heard she disguised herself as a peasant and fled Beijing hidden under rubbish in an ox cart."

That was indeed true. The foreign forces successfully combined to show what a real army can do when it's given the green light to lose control. They did famously in the countryside, far from the Forbidden City, but created such terror in Beijing itself that they got everything they wanted, plus war reparations fit to cripple China, as if China weren't already broken.

The ambassador's eyes were unfocused. "All the Qing's horses," he mused.

"And all the King's men," piped up Pericles proudly, so thankful to his mother for teaching him something that he could contribute.

THE NEXT MORNING "MISS Lily Chin," said Myra Hoolihan. "Meet Lily Ambrose."

"Delighted, I'm sure," said the tall, neatly dressed woman.

"Mrs Ambrose was known as the finest bloom north of 'Frisco."

"Myra!" blushed the old pro.

"You're still very lovely," said Lily, quite truthfully.

"Miss Chin here needs some lessons in repelling unwanted advances," said Myra. "I can only teach her so much about scrapping. You know the subtle stuff."

Within a week, the young lady learned not only how to do the mashed potato to a man's nuts, but how to evade the drugged handkerchief, how to slip away, slide out of, and identify the sly sneak-up as well as the grab. And how to play dead or not worth playing with or killing, *if it we goddamn hope not, comes to that.*

She was an obedient, respectful, and joyful student. "The daughter I never had," sighed Myra to her old friend Lily, or maybe it was the other way.

They were frantic to teach her well. They taught her how valuable she was as a prize, how likely she was to be kidnapped. Every time she left the Hoolihan establishment, she was shadowed by a Hoolihan, the sons even coming to blows between them, for the privilege.

With her looks and obvious breeding, this exotic flower was liable to be picked to be kept in the finest of backrooms. "I heard tell that the President has one a those," said Lily Ambrose to Myra Hoolihan.

"I hadn't never heard that. But it sure sounds true. A gilded cage! Now I know what it means." Of course they didn't tell the girl. They didn't want to scare her. Just prepare her.

On her 'graduation' day, Lily Ambrose gave her a battered cigar box. "From my golden days."

Of all the precious curios that Ambassador Jin had been given and traded for the two of them to be able to live, nothing had approached the strange beauty and practical attraction of this.

The box was lined with red velvet. On it lay a set of gloves of silk knit so fine you could hardly feel the fabric. The gloves were crafted with hundreds of invisible slits, and lined gossamer, yet it wasn't. It was, incredibly, blowfish skin, worked by a special pull string. Worn normally, they were a set of elegant gloves in the most tasteful shade of pearl. In peril, pull the strings and they were gloves of deadly spines, one scratch from which could paralyse. One light grip, not even a grab, could cause the most agonizing, lingering death.

"Put 'em on."

They fit as if tailor-made. "Mind you be like them," said Lily Ambrose. "Look at them things. They look like saying boo would make 'em fall to pieces, yet they ud rip the balls, excuse me, outta a bad man. A plenty bad, bad world out there, come to think of it. Just give 'em the go."

Father and daughter broke hearts once again when they left.

ONWARDS THEY TRAVELLED AS the world roiled ever angrier. They seemed to be relatively safe on the move—safe enough to design further dangerous adventures for their pleasure and to keep theoretically on their toes, just as before. But Jin Youwei wasn't as happy. He had started to resemble more and more, an English amateur-troop actor of Hong Kong, circa 1901. They kept flitting from place to place and she learned from each one. He exclaimed over new discoveries, languages, horrible foods that were strangely prized, customs that were 'normal'.

And everywhere, increasingly, like some badly written play, he sighed as if something were coming, something that had to come, something that was so obviously coming that you didn't *care* any more. He sighed so much that one day she lost her temper. "It is *not* nothing!" she said. They were in Sarajevo then.

He swallowed his hunk of hard cheese. "I miss China terribly."

Sometimes, she thought, wanting to box his ears. "It's 1912 already. The Qing dynasty is a dodo. There is no reason to stay *here*, and every reason to go home."

"Home?"

"Wouldn't you like to hear people speaking a language that values tones?"

They took the first boat back.

THEY LANDED IN SHANGHAI. Exciting, confusing, thrilling, brooding, doomed. They didn't stay long. He still had the travel bug, but his joy in travel, his essential mischievousness, was missing, as if he'd forgotten it on some overnight stop. They moved around more than ever before. He was both purposeless and driven.

And Beijing? She'd assumed he'd want to go there first, but he avoided it. One evening she challenged him.

"That great bowl of intrigue," he answered. "Why there?"

"To see your picture behind a bowl of mandarin oranges."

"Ha!"

But she wouldn't be put off. As inscrutable things happen, some years after his execution, he had been awarded a posthumous Honour of Bravery. They had heard that someone had erected a shrine.

For her, he made the trip. He didn't want to see anyone from before, didn't want to find out who was dead, who had survived, or how. What tore his heart the most was the loss of something he could not admit, people being supposedly the most important. In the midst of the disastrous Boxer Rebellion, something irreplaceable had been wantonly destroyed in Beijing. The Hanlin Library, China's greatest repository of books and learning, had been torched, to go the way of the Library of Alexandria.

He kept that tragedy to himself and accompanied her on this fool's errand, with good enough cheer. She wouldn't find anything, they'd spend a day in the city and they'd be on their way.

But there it was. The day was so cold that white clouds coming from mouths brightened the brown smog from charcoal fires. The shrine was meticulously carved of granite, with sayings in a dozen languages. The carver must have almost gone mad copying each mark, for he was illiterate. No joss sticks burned but there was indeed, a bowl of mandarin oranges, so fresh their scent prickled the inside of her nose.

A man was arranging them. He had the bearing and dress of a top civil servant, one who'd been promoted on merit more than connections.

This was the same man we met earlier who had taken guidance from the wax head of his hero.

He knelt and said a few unintelligible words, and was rising to go when he felt a hand touch his shoulder. He knew who it was without turning. He had always hoped this would happen, and now knew this would not be the only time the ghost of Jin Youwei would come to him.

Without insulting the ghost by raising his eyes to the apparition, he rushed away though he wanted with every fibre of his soul to look upon his idol. Every day he had talked to the head, had asked it if there was any reason to things that happen. In the tumultuous days the Ambassador had predicted, so much had changed. Two events happened on the same day, which changed this lowest-level civil servant translator's life. He was called into his superior's office and given that position, possibly at the very hour that three drunk soldiers broke into his house and accidentally burnt it to rubble. His wife had successfully hidden from them, in the house.

JIN YOUWEI DID NOT want to see his ancestral home, had been extremely careful through the years to stay ignorant as to the whereabouts of his wife and four sons. Alive or dead, he wanted nothing to do with that past.

Father and daughter left Beijing on the wings of its dirty dawn.

They travelled on. Ever on. Through cities, towns, villages, deserted grasslands, up through passes where from his comments and caution, she couldn't tell which was more dangerous—the thin and slippery road and its precipitous drop, or the bandits.

They travelled by any means available—carriage, sedan, cart, foot; by beasts of burden from steamhorse to ass, ox, and man.

It was an adventure. China was indeed, bigger than the world. She was glad they had returned, loved hearing and speaking so many tongues. But he was often tired and she would have said listless but there was something else. She couldn't get it out of him.

One afternoon, he turned unaccountably perky. Pointing theatrically, he shouted at the top of his voice (the only way he could be heard) the famous song, 'Only Immortals come down to the world from Mount Jiajing'.

She looked out from under their tarp.

No wonder they don't call it their Forbidden City, she thought crankily, *Who else would want to live up there?* At some other time she might appreciate that peak hidden by black clouds. At the moment, there was a far more welcome sight: the small town the forbidding mount loomed over. They had just reached its once-paved edge. The place was obviously an ancient roadstop on a route once important some long-forgotten time ago.

The cart's horses needed shelter. Unlike their driver who had covered his head and shoulders with a woven pine-needle cape, their heads and backs were bare. It was late May, and the sky was pelting spring hailstones big as a man's fist, louder than a clapping audience.

She was comfortable enough in her poor but warm clothing of padded cotton covered with a belted sheepskin, and cloth and straw boots stuffed with whatever they could get—grass, rags, cotton, wool. She needn't stop for herself. But couldn't the horses shelter and rest—and wouldn't it be nice to stay the night before going onwards to—where? She couldn't imagine, for the road looked to go straight to the mountain's base.

Her father leaned out and touched the driver's hunched shoulder just as another volley of hail crashed down. "Stop," he yelled out.

The driver thought he was crazy. Well, crazier than before. There was no way he was going to stop here with no shelter, not when there was an inn just a quarter *li* away. The driver had had enough. This idiot had stupidly already paid, so he could find his own way from here on. He jumped off his seat, went around to the back of the cart, threw off the tarp and manhandled all the luggage out onto the broken paving stones.

The crazyman stood watching, smiling and nodding. The driver almost pitied the man's beautiful daughter, but life had so hardened him, he couldn't afford to feel for his own horses.

JIN YOUWEI POUNDED ON the nearest door.

Bang bang! Bang bang bang. Bang!

The hail was louder than ever. Three times he repeated the sequence, and finally, the other side of the door creaked with locks being opened.

He turned to his daughter, mouthing, "Home."

IN BEING DRAWN 'HOME', of course Jin Youwei hadn't thought of this town, or the house which he'd only slept in one night—as truly 'home'. He had no home. He had only said that to his daughter because she had none either, and he was unaccountably tired, lost, and needed to say something positive. They would move on tomorrow and he would forgive his memory for its perfidy, for *what is memory but an organ of the mind that delights in tricking the weary and nostalgic?*

So many years before, he had set up this place as one of his contingency planning pieces. He'd been on his way to somewhere and found the town uncommonly charming—that was what he told himself but he'd never noticed the town. It was the ridiculously misplaced little publishing house fronted by a mouthwatering bookshop that made him stop. He dumped his bags by the door and was instantly enfolded into the embrace of the shop's stock, so much so, he didn't notice night had fallen till he rubbed his eyes, trying to focus.

"There," said a voice from a back room, its door closed. "Behind you. Tea, rice, bed."

He looked around, and sure enough, someone, the owner? had made enough space between piles of books for a small table, an oil lamp, a pot of fragrant *pu erh* tea and a cup, and a plate holding one stale rice ball and a pickled turnip as grizzled and yellow as if it had been freshly sliced from an old man's head.

That night he had the best sleep of his life, for he dreamt he lived here, and the place was run by the poet himself, Li Bao. They drank wine and tea together and the poet wrote, sang his poems and discussed with his humble acolyte, Jin Youwei, centuries of conundrums.

The next morning he had no choice but to leave. The shop owner/publisher was nowhere in sight, nor, come to think of it, had he ever been.

Jin Youwei wanted to thank him, and was curious to meet him. It would be crass and rude to leave something, even a message. But Jin Youwei was already late for a very important date, a hard 80 *li* trip away, the first part by ox or pack donkeys. *The bookseller/publisher will need to know I will return.* That was what he told himself. He could not leave without clawing a foothold here.

The owner of the house next door was sitting outside, his eyes and mouth pulled down by a life's worth of sadness.

Jin Youwei bowed to him and with a magician's flourish, produced a large mottled grey 100-year-old egg.

"Please," he said. "As a gesture of my sincerity. Let me crack it open for you."

He did something with his thumbs and it began to open, but instead of the rank reek of preserved duck egg, there arose a beatifically smiling Guanyin in scentless caterpillar-green jade.

The man jumped up as if someone had burnt his bum. The statue could have been made of dung for all he cared. She'd come to him. That was all that mattered.

Guanyin, immortal goddess of love and mercy, had met her mark.

When Jin Youwei recognized the man's reaction, he had to adjust his planned negotiations from a straight trade of a curio to being the Immortal's emissary, a go-between. The goddess would stay with this man who'd been so sad, light his life by her presence and guard him as forever as he lived. In return, the house would belong to the emissary. And, *thank Guanyin for this!* The former owner was being allowed to stay as housekeeper indefinitely, for the mysterious Mr _____ (the old owner never did catch the name) travelled much, and would arrive unexpectedly. Since the region could be highly dangerous, the old owner would only open the front door at their secret code.

IT HAD BEEN YEARS, but when the arrival happened, the housekeeper proved to have done his job, and the little green ever-hatching Guanyin must have done hers. He was spry as a ferret, and bustled about immediately to make beds ready for the exalted one and his young companion. Did the owner look the same as before? Neither could remember, nor could they remember the name, not that the housekeeper cared. He'd only ever had eyes for Guanyin.

It had been a long and not-what-any-doctor-would-order journey so far, with so many changes of persona and lessons about avoiding (or were those prudent lessons in avoidance actually master classes in flirtations with?) death. And as Jin Youwei's little daughter grew up, sometimes he had no idea who was leading whom in that wish to wave a red flag within snort-range of a bull.

Jin Libao, now nineteen, had a talent that sometimes tired her father, who had almost forgotten his old staid loves, his admittedly dry passions, mildew-scented, as he fell under the influence of his daughter's demands to keep up with his own requirements to travel in disguise, to constantly throw any dogging snoopers off their scent. Tea merchant and servant, dangerously slimy mandarin on a fact-finding tour with his little peach, The Felonious Sleight of Truth Magic act, two poor musicians...

Both father and daughter should have been exhausted, wishing only to scrub off the dust of the journey, soak in a petal-strewn bath, and sleep. The bowlegged housekeeper scurried off as fast as he could, to boil water.

"That can wait," called Jin Youwei, who couldn't wait to step next door.

THE BOOKSTORE WAS MORE tempting than ever. Exquisitely refined treatises in many types of book forms, including slats of rarest wood and paper made of mulberry, kelp, hemp, cotton, the inside lining of snakeskin—and for a 700-year-old book on etiquette, what he'd read of but never seen: the smoothest age-defying pages made from pounding the silk robes of those fallen into disrepute. Wonderfully obese omnibuses. Geographies teeming with dragons and mountains whose tops were inhabited by Immortals. Works that spanned the world in this little shadow of a stop along the road.

Father and daughter roamed the shelves, the floor, the piles, the trestle tables. All his bookish avariciousness rose in his soul like the devil rising in the breast of a missionary who has never known other than the literary meaning of *breast*.

The place was a veritable catacombs.

He found nooks he'd not remembered before, objects of worship he'd only heard tell of. The tray of well-used 1000-year-old clay type. A pillar of carved wooden page blocks for an early Qing period book on morality. And that lump hidden under a casually tossed, dust-velvetted silk cloth couldn't be, but something deep inside him, something preternatural, confirmed the impossible to be true. Under that silk *was* the actual *Chunqui*, the *Spring and Autumn Annals* written by Confucius himself and said to have been burnt in the 'burning books and burying Confucian scholars' campaign launched by Qin Shi Huang, the first emperor of China.

His face flushed, his heart fluttered. The smells of pages opened after ages almost drove him insane with lust.

All of a sudden, he remembered his daughter who he had brought in to introduce her to the illicit delights of physical collection. "I used to have books like these," he said, with a touch of braggadocio.

"Mn," she said, if she said anything.

Hurt, he took his eyes from all this precious stuff and turned to her.

She had her back to him. She only had eyes for the back room.

To be specific, what was standing in the doorway so close she could touch him though she was out of his line of vision.

"Can I help you?" he said quite rudely to her father (which must be the first recorded instance of the proto-'Excuse *me*').

JIN LIBAO HAD ALWAYS loved her father, and men had pestered her with declarations of love for years. Their shallow passions, their unwarranted self-confidence, their worship when they knew nothing about her—disgusted her. She'd had so many proposals of marriage, she'd lost count. She'd had to use her gloves twice, once with gloriously fatal consequences.

But this imperious feeling she had about this carelessly dressed man was, she knew in the pit of her stomach, something she'd never felt before. It was—

Ridiculous.

Unreasonable.

Unbelievable.

Illogical.

Positively mythical.

And it demanded to be obeyed. It was irrational, but if she'd learned one thing from her father, it was—*Imperious decrees are never rational.*

This man framed by the doorway to an Ali Baba cave of a back room smelled like her father, but with something irresistibly extra—the scent of a man of the mind who works with his hands: glue, ink, and the musk of calligraphy brushes.

His learnedness, curiosity, calligraphic skills, those impractical poet eyes, that decadent undercurrent of the collector—he radiated them as an aura.

Those hands captivated her. The veins stood proud of the shiny sandalwood-coloured skin. That they were strong hands was obvious. The back room was filled with heavy printer's equipment—presses, plates in wood and metal, type, binding machines. Mountains of printed books and paper yearning to be inked by stamp and paintbrush. His fingers didn't look just strong, but sensitive.

And what clinched the irresistibility—those four white hairs jutting from his chin. He was *it*. Her whole being said this, and to think she hadn't been looking or feeling the need.

That he was older than her father was piffle. His face, including those laugh lines, evinced an ageless vitality quite missing in the mien of so many young men of high breeding and infinite ignorance, who pretended world weariness while being merely terrifically boring.

She knew they'd be compatible. A not-so-faint stench of burnt rice wafted out from the back room.

It was plain as an unadorned wall to her father, who was struck so hard by the sight, he couldn't speak.

It was love at first sight for him too. *If Li Bao had been dragged from posterity and plopped here, this is who he would be.*

How can I stand in her way? I'd marry him myself if I could.

LOVE DIDN'T HAPPEN IN the first minute to the bibliophile bachelor or widower (the father assumed widower while the daughter didn't think to ask) publisher-poet Zhang Gong, but love *did* happen, to the joy of love-sick Jin Libao and the mixed feelings of her father. *Who knows how long he will last? Love might never come, so seize it on the wing if you're lucky enough to recognize it flying by your life.*

And thus it was that before the moon waned, Zhang Gong wed the young, beauteous polyglot mistress of disguise and mediocre juggling skills, Jin Libao, and she moved into his crowded backroom workshop where they made a bit more space on the floor for their sleeping pad at night.

Her father, next door, fought his better selves but the fight was hopeless—like putting your finger to your lips to get a kettle to stop screaming. Not only did he yearn to sit at the feet of this reincarnation of his idol, but his collector's soul hurt. *Hurt*, from starvation. He could go next door any time he wanted. He could sleep beside the shelves, bivouac under the presses, curl up on paper-bundle mattresses, for their owner was infinitely amenable. "I love your books," said the ex-collector. "I love my books, too," said the bookseller. "I don't know how you can live without them over there. Every time I sell a book, I mourn its loss." Zhang Gong was an unreformed addict, all right.

Indeed, for the man with the vast library in his head, the lusty temptations of corporal clutching—to have and to hold—and the scents evinced by works warming at his touch, and yes, it should have been a cliché but he was beyond shame—the sibilant sound of sheets—were almost too great. Only love conquered them—love for his daughter.

She had been his great love, his Precious, and it seemed to his lesser self that it was mightily unfair for her to have the remarkable and ageless Zhang Gong and all these books, *and* possibly in short order, the prize that would eclipse all—a child who would possess in one package his own reformed self, the accomplished prodigy who was his lovable daughter, *and* that infinitely wise bibliophile publisher who was Li Bao reincarnate.

AS TO THE BIBLIOPHILE publisher, that he *was* Li Bao was a secret the ancient poet yearned to share, but dared not. Nor could he rise above his human faults to admit to his wife and her father how he must have inadvertently bewitched her by his very venerableness. *I didn't try to!* Indeed, he had thought himself well hid, for he had been such a profligate irresistible as the famous poet that he had always tried to burrow since, not wanting to take advantage of anyone.

But the daughter was indeed, so lovable, wise, and knowledgeable; and her father that man who he'd watched so many years before, and wanted keenly then, to kidnap and keep as a drinking and poetry companion. And here he was again, even more fascinating. Li Bao's inner eye had 20/20 vision, especially looking backwards. For at least 150 years, he had not felt such companionship with another man— but that was nothing compared to the love growing inside him for *her*. Not since... No. He had *never* felt like this. He looked back on his ancient love poems and could only laugh at them. Those former feelings might as well have been for radishes.

A WEEK AFTER THE wedding, a bulbous-nosed trader in bezoars left town though he'd never entered it.

A whole two days later (love isn't always blind, but it does have tunnel vision) Jin Libao noticed that her father wasn't hanging around, and wasn't sick in bed next door. The housekeeper knew nothing, but then admitted he'd seen something. He had been bribed so well, he swore her father had disappeared, with his bags and cases, in a blue puff of smoke.

Jin Libao didn't know what she felt more— heartbroken grief, abandonment, thankfulness at his grace in not crowding their love, or this irrepressible need to giggle. It was hard to tell what she was doing by the time it ended in hiccups. *You weak old rogue*, she thought. *You thought you were ready to settle down, but you couldn't resist the pull of those three sirens: Dangerous New Experience.*

He'd left a note: "Never forget your gloves."

IT WASN'T THE NEXT year, nor the year after that, but eventually, after two miscarriages, in 1919, the married couple had a child. They named her Zhang Ouyang, after Ouyang Xiu, the great Song dynasty's poet/archaeologist/historian who had also been a top civil servant. The child's parents had talked through several nights about a name, and the result had been much less literary than Zhang had expected. He stroked his white hairs and decided that his loving wife's first love must have been her father, who was obviously more accomplished than he would ever be.

The revelation didn't hurt. Rather, he respected her for it, and felt privileged to be tossed the merest crumbs of her love. He was a slow burner, but he did burn. He hated the baby while it grew in her. If it killed her, he would kill it.

By the time the baby was born, he was so in love with his wife, it pained him to think of her suffering in any way. He was frightened of life, for her. He lived every day in a kind of fever of mixed love and fear. "Of all the wives I've ever had," he almost told her one night, "and all the children over the centuries, I've never been in love as I am with you."

Perhaps he was too wise to say anything. Perhaps he was too unwise. He was wise enough to know he couldn't change the past, turn back the clock to the time before clocks, when he had been given with all good intentions, his life-cycle changing nightly dose of immortality mushroom. He could only make the best of this possibly interminable stage of life. Certainly, he had never expected this gift to fall upon him, this so-called Luck.

The baby didn't kill her. It was an extension of her—of them. They both delighted in little Zhang Ouyang, and in each other.

Meanwhile, the world outside the shop bubbled, and boiled over. The times were getting more and more frightening. Rumours spread. Warlords sang with joy, generals sent in troops, bandits struck like black-garbed lightning. Teaching their child was an escape for them both, and they taught her so many things unsuitable for children. By the time she was seven, she could speak like a native from so many places, and imitate so many people, you'd think she was a genius parrot, but they didn't allow her to speak a language unless she understood it first. She learned dexterity from her father, who could set type no larger than fly spat. She learned diplomacy and disguise from her mother. She learned great love from both.

The streets became increasingly unsafe. The news was more unsettling than ever. This town, which was usually safely out of the way on the road, was now *on the road.*

Jin Libao half-wished her father were around. He might have been able to teach Zhang Gong the value of the library of the mind, to teach him how much of a danger all these beautiful books were, *these possessions that tie you down.*

She itched to disguise her little family and manage their escape. She knew she could make a new life for them all somewhere safe. She must have inherited that sense that had kept her father alive through all his diplomacies. Her husband didn't have the skills. *And why should he? I should convince him we should all leave. But his books. His workshop. He loves them too much to leave.* How she yearned to protect him, and their extraordinary daughter!

If only he had known. He had grown gaunt and feeble from worry. All night long he hatched mad schemes to escape, go to a foreign land. But he had lived in this room or its precursors for centuries, so long that he felt no confidence about flying out the door. He was such a learned man, so full of theories about the world, but *what good does that do? My books? All this? How can anyone be tied by possessions at a time like this?*

"SHE CAN SPEAK SIX dialects as well as Japanese and Russian, read and write anything, and handle your communications equipment with more care than anyone else. She is also good at juggling, graceful and sneaky as a snake. I have prepared her well."

Her mother, Jin Libao, carrying two buckets of water in her bare hands, had been swept up five days before in a warlord raid and played with drunkenly till she wasn't any fun. Generalissimo Chiang's approaching Guomindang had a better reputation—for cold-blooded professional murder. There was nowhere to hide, and her father's skills were only of use if knowledge were power. He would have laughed bitterly at *The pen is mightier than the sword*. So he didn't try to hide when the Red Army marched in. Instead, he sought out the commander, told him how valuable this girl would be to him, and why such a powerful man should protect her personally.

The commander hadn't slept for three days. The army had been slithering its march at night for its protection, a balance act to command. Treacherous, slick terrain in the dead of night or the day's bullets, bombs, and bayonets.

The commander was so exhausted his ears rang, yet he didn't kick the old man out of his way or laugh, hearing the ludicrous description of this little prodigy. She was just a child, and a frail one at that. *So sad*, he thought, *the desperation a parent can go to*. But this old man had an auspicious chin, four white hairs jutting out like shining swords—and the girl was so tender— as likely to reach maturity as a tomato growing by the road.

"Her name," the old man said, "is Zhang Dingtianlidi." Zhang Ouyang glanced up at her father, but said nothing. He'd stripped her of the name he and her mother had given her. She hurt for herself, for him, for the spirit of her mother. However, *Father is right*. Being named after a great Tang dynasty poet could be a death sentence now.

Dingtianlidi. Indomitable Spirit, indeed, thought the commander. *What balls!* Imagine, hanging that title— not a proper name at all—on a child.

Yet the commander was so demoralized and frankly, frightened for his life, on this supposed attack that was turning into a horrifically incompetent retreat.

The Communists had no time for superstition, but he didn't hesitate. "I will protect her, professor Zhang." He wanted Indomitable Spirit to protect *him*. It was 1934. She was thirteen.

Old Zhang hadn't been lying. Little Zhang Dingtianlidi with her progressive name that so inspired people, gave them heart, distinguished herself time and again for her bravery and her unbelievable skills. And she found languages as easy to pick up as chopsticks. Though she couldn't carry the communications box, she was the only one who could use it with any speed and accuracy. Like the other Little Red Devils, as all the children who did grown-up jobs on that campaign were called, she didn't cry nor could she tell anyone how much she missed her family.

Her father, in their last hour together before he took her to the commander, sat her before him in the back room, folded her hands in her lap, and folded his in his.

He told her that their grief was a precious jewel that only belonged to them—a treasure that would never be lost but only shined when it wasn't exposed to others. "Your outward appearance must be like a chestnut, catching shine but showing nothing of what's within. Show feelings of love for someone only if you want to hurt them."

Then he said, "I am the past," and told her the story of the girl who got lost trying to find her way back to yesterday.

THE COMMANDER WAS GOOD as his word, putting her under his personal protection. Soon rumour spread that Indomitable Spirit was his little kumquat, for wherever they were bivouacked, he managed to retire privately with her to sleep. This certainly kept her from being taken by anyone else.

He 'slept' with an arm wrapped tightly around her, his body at an awkward tilt so his jacket buttons wouldn't dig into her back.

At this period, the dangers of night marching were too great, so the column had to sleep when darkness fell. By the third night, she knew when he actually slept, because he, normally morosely quiet, talked. Things like "There's nothing here, can't you see?" and "Chiang has it, warehouses of it" and "Provisioning *you* the highest priority?" Then "*Take* my money. See what good it'll do you." His tones grew increasingly high-pitched, desperate. "Please leave me, or I'll be joining you... yes, then I'll agree priorities."

Then the sobs would come, and finally, the spasmic kick which always woke him. He'd apologize profusely for kicking, settle himself against her again, and try so hard to be considerate that she could hear his every shuddering breath, feel the ridges of his crumpled uniform pants, stiff with grime—till it was time to wake or he exhausted himself again, and another one-sided conversation/begging session began.

On the fourth night, he yelled something that sounded like "Keep away!" and caught her chin in such a sharp uppercut that he woke. He wouldn't stop saying *sorry*. He'd had no idea that he talked in his sleep, but that last scene was too fresh in his mind to be denied. And he believed her when she repeated the other things she'd heard him say.

"Can you sleep?" he said. He was standing, bent over her, bathing her chin with a rag moistened in his cold tea. "I'll be on the floor over there."

She pushed his hand away and sat up.

"I swear I didn't mean to harm you." He kept running a hand through his sweat-matted hair. "I'll stay there. You'll be safe from everyone, including me."

"From people, I already know. From *you*—" She laughed like muffled cat-bell. "I am Indomitable Spirit. Bring up and push out your dreams. No bad dream can stand up to me."

She looked so sure of herself, so strong, even with that lump growing on her jaw.

Tell her, said his cowardly self. *Unburden yourself*. His nobler spirit resisted, but his need was too strong. Besides, *she is strong enough*, he was sure. He didn't believe in Guanyin or any old goddess, but this girl—*I believe in her*.

He still had enough nobility in him that he would have resisted, but for one thing.

He'd punched her, fighting to protect her. They were probably laughing.

"These aren't dreams."

HE TOLD HER ABOUT them coming as soon as he laid his head down. They wouldn't leave him alone. They wanted what he could not give, or what he would not give. He beat around the bush there until he blurted out that some wanted *her*. She couldn't believe that. It was obvious to her that wherever she went, people whispered. The commander was loved and respected. She had full confidence, even when she walked amongst the lowliest of recruits.

Exasperated, he tried again. "I am glad that you feel some protection when amongst our troops. And I will protect you with my life as much as possible in action. But this is nothing compared with the true masses. The Party cares nothing for the real masses."

She was shocked, but not as much as he, that he'd blurted this out. "They're what you'd call ghosts, child."

"Ghosts?" Unconscious of the pretty picture she made, she put her hand to her mouth to stifle a giggle.

She had learned about ghosts from her parents. She would never forget their joint performance, just for her, of *Peony Pavilion*, Tang Xianzu's once-popular play. A daughter of a high official is in love with a young man, a scholar, who of course she can only dream about till she dies, her longing for him unrequited. But before she dies, she's energetic enough to plan ahead in a most silly manner. She buries not herself, but a portrait of herself in the garden. The young scholar quite naturally goes to the garden and throws himself and his poor but tasteful robes on the dirt between two persimmon trees, where he scrabbles barehanded for no reason, until lo! He uncovers her portrait and is laid low in awe at the painted beauty. What timing, she thinks. She forgives him, of course, and tells him to open her coffin. He does, and voila! She's as beautiful and alive as when he'd been wasting too much time studying to notice her. They have some problems—inevitable with the dead who aren't dead—but all comes right in the end and the high official's family gain not just a son, but their once-dead daughter now restored, to the horror of her jealous sisters.

"My parents added that ending with the sisters," she told the commander, remembering her mother saying, "We have committed a crime performing this play this way for you," and her father adding "One of the three great truths is that nothing old is ever meant to be funny. And this is from the Ming Dynasty."

"What are the other two great truths?" she asked.

"You *should* say, 'Where are they?'"

"Where?"

"In hiding," said her father.

Other ghosts her parents talked about were also objects of fun. Some flew around throwing lethal stars at living throats. Some were matriarchs who made household hell. Or the grandfather ghost who loved congee so much, he fought mice to scrape it from the pot. Silly apparitions, nothing to be frightened of. *Believe in them as you believe in the immortality mushroom, daughter.*

The commander knew she wasn't trying to be disrespectful, but it was hard for him to maintain his faith.

She must have noticed his disappointment. She bowed her head. "Tell me, please. I am young and have not seen."

She was, indeed, surprisingly ignorant, even in this ignorant modern age. He had to teach her from the beginning, but he was patient and she tried to take it all in. How ghosts aren't anything to be afraid of, as such. That they're just another stage in life, like a butterfly breaking free of its chrysalis. "And if it's ripped violently into the next stage, uh, as happens with, say, ur, war..." His eyes avoided hers. "It needs extra care."

She only knew butterflies and their breaking free from literature, so they left that for another time.

"So you say ghosts exist," she said, "and they're nothing to be afraid of, *as such*." His forehead was shiny with sweat again. "Why are you so afraid?"

"Let's take a walk." He stuffed an envelope in his jacket, and opened the tent flap. The moon was a sliver. He led to the top of a rise, ordering the watch there to go down and sleep. Wetting a finger, he checked the wind. Smiling grimly, he pulled out the envelope, plucked out a red-coated stick, stuck it in the earth, and lit it.

"Bend down this way. Like *this*. Let the smoke show you."

He settled himself behind her, his arms reaching out as a protective cage.

They were *everywhere*—as far as she could see. She'd thought the numbers of people in this Long March to be overwhelming enough. But they were a sprinkle of rain lost in this vast flood. The joss smoke shifted, and all was as it had been.

"Why don't they come to me?" she asked.

"They would if they thought you could help them."

"What could they want?"

"What do any of us want?" He sounded irritated. "Enough to get by on, to have a halfway decent existence."

"*Them?*"

He opened and shut his mouth.

"Who would I tell?" she whispered. "I owe you my life."

She knew so much, he'd forgotten how little she must know, this sheltered beloved.

"Well," he said, muffling his voice. "Just imagine you're a member of the Central Committee. You think 'All food belongs to the People' so the food is taken for the People. You can't picture the peasant family having all their food taken from them, as well as their land and their means to make food. They now have nothing. To survive, they must depend upon the People. But suddenly there are so many like them, they are a burden on the productive people. All the planners, fighters, people in the cities, people who matter, need to be fed—"

"And they're so many more than you and me, but we are the ones who we see?"

"The ghosts would be pleased you understand," he smiled. "But this must be our secret."

"Of course! But do those peasants need money? Didn't they have no money before?"

He was exasperated for a moment, till he remembered. She was wise beyond her years, and so ignorant. "If you have nothing," he said, "Money's the only way to get anything."

"For ghosts?"

"Especially."

"They need money to live? Well, not live but."

She was beginning to understand.

"But why don't they just steal your money, steal from the Party's treasury? What do they want from *you?*"

"To them, our notes and coins are play money, even if we had enough of it to satisfy them here. I haven't seen much money, have you?" He pulled out a dirt-grey note. "This'll buy half a cabbage leaf. And anyway, it hasn't gone through the stage it must, to be legal tender."

"But why do you keep telling them to see Generalissimo Chiang?"

"He's got storehouses filled to bursting with money for the... the... "

"Dead?"

"Shh. They feel insulted by that term. It lessens them. The caterpillar isn't dead when it's a butterfly."

"All this worry about them taking offence." She *hmph*ed, her immature look and sound quite unintentionally comical—a pint-size queen in uglifying rags. "They haven't treated *you* with the respect you deserve. They're just ghosts, whether they like it or not."

He nodded, beaten.

"Like pulling thread from a carrot! What *is* the problem? Just attack Chiang, open the vaults and let the ghosts in to take their money! Wouldn't that solve your problem?"

Indomitable Spirit! He laughed till his stomach hurt.

She felt a gust behind her, and a certain light stink. The commander reached for her hand.

They'd come tumbling out of the joss-stick smoke—a one-eyed brigand waving a bloodthirsty knife, and an officer she thought she remembered for his rather silly face, his jacket crusted black.

"So you brought her at last," said the brigand.

"Never," said the commander.

"You heard him," said the officer.

The brigand threw the officer to the ground.

The officer bashed a revolver against the brigand's head.

The brigand lifted a knife and stabbed the officer sewing-machine style, downupdownupdown—as the commander tightened his grip on the girl till he felt her relax.

She looked at him, not ready to believe her eyes. "They can't draw blood."

"Right."

As they watched, the combatants tired themselves out, dusted themselves off, and walked away.

"And their feet don't quite meet the ground."

"As yours won't. One thing we can look forward to."

"So why does the brigand want me? I'm not money."

He blushed. "You're as good as money, if. . . "

She had a horrible vision of being prepared, of the stink of her being burnt. "Thank you for saving me."

"Captain Wu would have died for you again, if he could."

"Please thank him if you see him again. He must be awfully frustrated."

"At least he can probably sleep," he said lightly.

"Do they sleep?"

He shrugged. "We'll find out soon enough."

THE NEXT NIGHT SHE was waiting for whoever came. She still needed joss-stick smoke to see them, but that was neither here nor there. She seized the day, so to speak. As she explained (he never had, thinking it obvious, but each stage of life has its own priorities and obsessions)—"The Commander and this whole column of the March would eagerly take the Generalissimo's warehouses for you, and for ourselves. We need food, medicine, ammunition—and we're adding to your numbers every day."

"You can trade for what you need," said a half-dressed officer. "What do we have to trade?"

He was probably desperate for ghost medicine. His injuries made her understand for the first time, how important money would be. *Just like the living, ghosts need money for bribes.*

She explained that the Commander would do his best to get ordered to take the Generalissimo's warehouses. If he was fortunate enough to be ordered there in this chaotic war, she would personally supervise the operation. She promised that not only would every note be burnt to a properly smoking crisp. The blasts would shoot the ash into the sky high enough to rain down money on the many multitudes in need.

The Commander did his best.

O, she was a heroine. Her name was loudly sung by a ghostly host.

She protected the commander from them, and from his fears, but could only do so much for so long. After this campaign that he hadn't expected to survive, his little ward was immediately assigned to a prestigious work unit in Beijing. They knew they couldn't write to each other, so she worried about him briefly, but she was too young to think of him for long—until too many years had passed.

One day she had to walk through an unfamiliar district. On a decrepit street, she noticed a doorless dark space little larger than a noodle stall of the old days. It was a temple, as filthy and disreputable as a beggar. Inside were two ancient women. She begged an illicit joss stick and stuck it in the sand beside theirs. Smoke curled just as she remembered. She peered through it, but either everyone was elsewhere, or they chose not to be seen.

That night in her sleep, she dreamed that the brave ghost of Captain Wu visited, and recited just for her:

>*Sea snail.*
>*Sea-snail shell.*
>*Sea-snail-shell sand.*

Perpetual immortality!

She had just asked whether it was by a classical poet, and seen his eyes drop in modesty, when she woke.

ALSO ON THE LONG MARCH was Zhang Chen (no relation. There are enough Zhangs in China to declare a good-sized country). Nineteen-year-old Zhang Chen enthusiastically enlisted to fight the corruption-ridden, fascist Guomindang, the thuggish warlords, bands of nothing-to-lose brigands, and all the other evil forces seething across the land—all killing for themselves. He saw, with the fine promises of the Communists and calls for the peasants to rise, an end to hunger, an end to oppression.

He, who was embarrassed at overstatement, sang love songs to the Party at the top of his voice. The promises they made were so progressive, the Cause so right, the Party so pure, even when it made the inevitable miscalculation.

For love, he didn't think to question why this march was so long. Why they had to go up and down the same deadly mountains and across the same grasslands—three terrible times. He suffered along with the others, eating grass and leather, having his feet turn into hard inhuman patchworked blobs coursed with ink-black veins.

During the march, he was only good for technical uses, machine fixing and all that, and would only be a scientist when peace prevailed, but he often thought of the great work of the composers of the love songs that so perfectly expressed what he, what *millions* felt about the Glorious Future being made.

After the march, that joy, fervour, wish to self-sacrifice for the Party filled his soul for years. The Party did make him into a scientist. He'd expected to be designing armaments—but agronomy was chosen for him, with a specialty of entomology. The only time he'd been in the countryside was during the march, but he threw himself into his studies and excelled, being snapped up to work in a shiny new institute in Beijing.

There, he worked diligently and surprised himself by becoming fascinated with the lives and social structures of insects and plants. He lived like a monk without thinking anything odd about that. He only had eyes for the Party. He thrilled to the Great Leap

Forward, forgiving it the lunacy of its romance with Lysenko's pseudoscience based on the wish that if plants were crowded together close enough, the urge to compete would be driven out of them and all would thrive. He kept his scorn for this nonsense to himself, thinking it would, like any squall, puff itself out.

But in mid 1959, he learned through whispers, the truth about the famine that was exterminating millions in the countryside. *They cover the fields like rice stubble out in Henan and Hebei provinces while the granaries are full to fulfil delivery targets—all to prove the new social biology a triumph.* Meanwhile, Beijing was gaily bannered, and at the cinemas, films of bumper harvests and shiny new tractors and trucks groaning with crops were almost sideshows next to the apple-cheeked men, women and children working with such joy in their hearts, they had to sing. Songs of glorious successes poured out of loudspeakers—songs so catchy, they infected people with earworms.

The day he caught himself humming 'Red Tide' at his cosy lab at the Institute, he dropped a flask, causing colleagues to look at him. He shrank into himself mentally—always on his guard to hide his guardedness.

Whispers about the famine were soon noisy as mice in a file cabinet, so the Party had to do something. The famine earned a series of euphemisms passed down from above. He was ordered to write a report putting the blame on nature, but he didn't do a good enough job. His next assignment was a paper for an international conference, detailing the glorious new yields in grains. One of his work unit colleagues was assigned to translate it into English, to be presented in Helsinki or somewhere. That colleague happened to be the woman he'd first seen as a heroic little girl on the Long March—Zhang Dingtianlidi.

In 1958, when the disaster began, she was assigned to his work unit at the Institute, to translate scientific papers into Chinese. And as he was tasked with helping to burnish the Party's shining reputation abroad, it was only natural that she was needed more and more by him to translate papers for him so that he could keep up with the failings of others so as to show in contrast how much the Party kept ahead.

They had met during the Long March but neither had appeared to notice the other. He didn't expect her to notice *him* but who hadn't heard of her, who hadn't wished to see her? There seemed to be nothing she wasn't capable of. In addition to her legendary intelligence and knowledge, she was also physically so brave, she gave others courage. Once she made her way down a mountain, alone, on a rainy night, to slip under the trucks of a Guomindang munitions and supply column and cut all their fuel lines—she thought up the plan and insisted on carrying it out alone. Some people said she was a towering statue of a woman. What a surprise to see reality.

At the Institute, they barely looked at each other. She was skilled at keeping her thoughts hidden, while he was naturally reserved, painfully shy, and anyway, would have been outraged were anyone to think he spent any energy on self-indulgent and wasteful romantic thoughts. (She had thought him not only handsome and unusually modest, but she admired his quick, sideways-thinking brains. He worshipped her, not just because of her reputation for bravery or her delicate beauty, but because her mind made him feel like a dullard.)

She was such a fast translator that she was worked quite hard. The extra loads of work caused by the famine would have been the undoing of any other translator. When another work unit tried to poach her, her unit's political officer called her in and advised her that she had a new duty to volunteer—to marry that scientist she did the most translations for. He was strange, it was true, but if she married him, she would be doing the most for her Party and her work unit.

She agreed dutifully, as did the scientist, neither showing any revealing enthusiasm. They officially joined later that day. There was no honeymoon or any decadent celebration, and the Party never suspected their private joy.

The Party wasn't the only party not suspecting the depths of Zhang Dingtianlidi's joy. She had never forgotten her father's instruction: *Your outward appearance must be like a chestnut, catching shine but showing nothing of what's within. Show feelings of love for others only if you want to hurt them.*

Her new husband would have thought her a mere Party match, cold and robotic, if they'd slept in separate rooms. But from their first night together, he knew that, if only he could strip her of her shell, she was warm inside as a roasted chestnut. He loved her with a fierce desperation. They never once spoke about their feelings, yet from that first night, she dropped off to sleep and he heard and felt what her sleep was—her arm wrapped around him, pulling him so close his shoulder cramped—her mouth moving—

those irregular breaths against his neck. Then "Not me."

"I didn't ask you for anything," he said. She must have felt him trying to get up, for her grip on him dug fingers into his ribs.

"Don't come here," she ordered.

It was all nonsense to him, but it always ended up with her begging so loud, he had to shove the pillow backwards into her face—and then pin her legs down with his own, or she'd kick herself awake. Every night. They didn't talk about this any more than they would have discussed their few moments of tender sex, always overly quiet in case anyone was listening on the other side of the wall. He so fiercely wanted to protect her that he wove a fantasy that he actually *could*.

So they were a married couple and they were able to stay up all night together whispering and writing notes they burnt, when she had to translate his latest assignment—the one detailing the glorious agricultural production boom of the Great Leap Forward. That they both failed at his latest assignment was probably an unavoidable natural disaster.

It was 1961. He was 46. She, 42.

They were stripped of their urban household registrations as well as any right of return for them, as well as the possibility of migration to the city for any child they might have. The names on their new documents read: *Zhang Chen* and *Zhang Ding*. She'd been stripped of her distinguishing *Dingtianlidi* because someone banished to the hinterlands needs to know she's been gutted of her so-called indomitable spirit. Whoever decided this must have had quite a sense of humour, because her husband, the disgraced scientist had been left with his given name, *Chen*—success.

They were sent to a collective farm in outer Henan Province.

THEY WERE PART OF a newly formed work unit of urbanites, all 'parasites', now manual labourers. Their first job was to gather up all the remains of the collective that had lived there till the year before— quite a test. It should have made a comrade stronger, more socialized. Reactionaries who still believed in ghosts shirked work or went mad, both convenient markers for elimination.

He earned a modicum of respect and security, for only he had any knowledge of agriculture and what life would be on the land, and his scientific work had given him a strong stomach.

They considered themselves relatively lucky. This collective farm was no longer part of the large Great Leap Forward commune originally of thirty thousand people, barracks, administrative/political building, and communal canteen. It was perched on a hillside, a little village of thirty mudbrick peasant cottages too insignificant to have bothered razing and placed too far away from the communal kitchen for the peasants to eat there, though their metal pots had been taken in the great smelting drive and their crops taken to help fulfil the impossible Five Year Plan.

The new inhabitants had to act like pioneers:

Firstly, building an administrative building for the cadre to live in and educate from.

Secondly, preparing the land anew and planting crops.

Luckily, they had been told that they could for each couple or family, pack a pot and a kettle. Their work unit would not set up a communal kitchen because it might make too much food. Instead, foodstuffs would be given out by the cadre assigned to their little collective farm.

THEY HAD BEEN DROPPED off by a truck as far as the dirt road went, an hour's walk away. Luckily again, said the two Long March veterans, the group had been supplied with enough food to last a season— millet, sorghum, dried turnips. Better than nothing, which they had expected, being told "you'll have to forage". And because of a kind and singularly brave colleague at the Institute, they had a good and varied supply of seeds. This was exceedingly lucky, for, other than some materials to build a new People's Palace of Fulfilment and Education, the government's effort in supplying these new farmers concentrated on their minds.

The building was designed in no time, thanks to the architect in the work unit. The building work was less efficient, the only members of the unit who had ever experienced true hardship and hands-on work being the two Long March veterans. Without discussing the matter, they both worked as clumsily as the rest of the work unit, for fear of sticking out. Other than the architect who announced his former profession as if they were all still members of society, no one else said anything about their former lives.

As soon as the building was finished, a team of three cadres arrived with all the skills to make sure their charges in the work unit developed and maintained correct thinking and vigour. This team lived in and worked from the Palace. Their arrival was celebrated because they carried with them a breeding sow and boar. There would be meat!

THE FARM WORK WAS brutal, as was only to be expected, but the biggest complaints most of the work unit had were about food, not that the smart ones dared complain.

There was never enough food, and all the best was always taken by the cadres in taxes. Pig breeding was a special work unit at the farm, because of course, the pigs were all for the nation, not the selfish wants of this insignificant collective farm that was really a prison for wrong-thinkers and reactionaries. Indeed, an early job was the building of a rudimentary road so that the cadres could come and go to the central office of the province, and army trucks could pick up the farm's fulfilments of the Plan.

The two Long March veterans (not that anyone but the cadres knew) were relatively untroubled by food. Her mother had trained her to be able to eat anything and practically nothing, so she'd been readied for the Long March's extremes. Zhang Chen hadn't been hardened as a child, but he toughened up on the march. So food bothered them intellectually more than physically. The question of who worked, who starved, distribution itself.

What they hungered for was books. They hadn't been allowed to bring any. Other than party political publications, all books were forbidden, for no Party member posted to such a place of exile would be at a high enough level to know what should be banned.

Every bit of intellectual stimulation had to come from each other's memories. He had never had his memory developed as she had, so was she or he worse off? They couldn't decide. The members of the collective might have stimulated each other if anyone could have afforded trust—they were all too poor for that.

In the first year, there were seven denunciations by work unit members of others in the unit, according to the political officer—each needing a public struggle session to start off with. Three sessions ended in work unit members being trucked away. One session earned a visit from an army unit, which carried out a quicker execution than members had been threatened with. It wasn't a case of mercy, just efficiency caused by soldiers not wanting to spend a moment more than necessary in this damned hellhole.

The couple were like two snails, each wanting to pull inside its whorl. But each felt it wrong to do that to the other.

Instead, in 1964, three years after they'd arrived, they had a child, guiltily, not knowing whether it was in unfounded optimism for the child's better future or their snatching of pleasure in creating something they could stimulate, enlighten. First, they gave him a protective shell. They called him *Wenge*, the most popular baby name that year. With 'Wenge' meaning 'Cultural Revolution', this new name vied with another praising Chairman Mao as the perceived safest.

ZHANG WENGE HAD NEVER seen anything beyond this brutal collective and its beastlike life. And if his parents didn't prepare him for escape, he never would. Even when he was on his mother's back while she worked in the fields, she talked to him. He was as fast a learner as she had been, his brain racing before he could walk. By the time he was three, he was learning at such a rate and with such hunger that it was hard to remember he was still almost a baby. They fed him science, nature, languages, even bourgeois cultural wonders and philosophies that were as useful at the collective farm and as likely for him to encounter here, as a pierced-work porcelain vase. In the dark each night and in the light of the moon, they would take turns giving him lessons.

From his father Zhang Chen, the lessons they both enjoyed the most were about the fascinating things that insects and other creatures do. How they live, what a plant feels when it takes up food and breathes. What eats what, what needs who. Science without myth. From his mother, reading and writing, classical and the ugly but non-elitist modern simplified, and so many languages that he'd be able to travel anywhere in China and talk like a native, including the centre of power, Beijing. She taught the boy to read and write English, but not to speak it. She who was classified 'fluent' had never had the chance to learn the spoken word of imperialism—too dangerous!

"All you learn you must keep secret," she said, but he must have picked that message up in his mother's milk, for he was a natural social fake. In their tiny mudbrick peasant hovel, they all three talked in barely audible whispers, and wrote only on their easily palmed dirt floor.

By age five, he was able to enjoy the lovely poetry of his grandfather, who had specialized in word paintings of such beauty, you could think horror never happened.

One winter night his mother recited a story that she called *The Dream of Han Tan*. Some irresponsible young man falls asleep when he should be watching a pot of millet. He dreams that he becomes not only accomplished, but a celebrated success. Inevitably, his accomplishments and success lead to being slandered and condemned to death. When he has thoroughly learned the worthlessness of his life, his crimes are wiped and he is promoted.

When the story ended, Zhang Chen silently clapped his hands. "That was such a silly story," he said to the boy. "Too silly to remember."

As soon as they settled him to sleep, Zhang Chen asked, "Why did you make up that dangerous rubbish?"

"I didn't make up anything," she bristled. "You, *of anyone*, should know it. Tang Xianzu. Back in the Ming dynasty."

"We should support each other."

"I handed you a light. You are blind."

That was the only bitter disagreement they ever had.

Not that they didn't disagree. She wanted to teach about ghosts. He was aghast.

"They exist to too many people for him to be ignorant of their beliefs," she said.

"Superstitious twaddle!"

Her second argument was a stroke of genius. "Ghosts will outlast the Party."

Therefore, their son learned the Two principles of Ghosts:

1) In many times and places, people say they've seen ghosts.

2) Because people say it's true is no reason to believe.

ZHANG CHEN, WHILE KEEPING up an outwardly positive attitude with his wife and son, drew into himself more and more. He took up a furtive pastime, a childhood passion that he'd been given by his grandfather, whose tales he grew out of as he grew into being a scientist. But hoeing weeds in the cornfield one day, he turned up a pebble and cleaned its face, and then he knew his grandfather wasn't lying about their existence. As to their powers, he was still a scientist, but he took to collecting them secretly, and hiding his finds from everyone. Not that he had the opportunity to give his little family a better life.

Instead, he made a tiny pair of very sharp scissors and cut intricate designs into corn husks for the pleasure of his wife and cultural education of his son. His mother had excelled at this art, but he was an amateur. Still, this was a bit of light-hearted, rare joy the three of them could have, before the artwork was burnt lest anyone else see.

Zhang Chen never let anyone know his despairs and hopes, especially his wife who he could not think of anymore as Dingtianlidi—Indomitable Spirit. He felt so tender toward and so guilty about her, he barely said a word to her and turned his face away in case she caught his eye, for it would only have made life more painful for her who had been turned by the system into an inferior form of hoe. Both of them were private as everyone in the village was, but they also had a reputation for kindness which, as time passed, was increasingly taken advantage of by the other members of the work unit who'd come out here no worse off than them.

Husband and wife each despaired deeply and ever more secretly as their son blossomed. One night while her husband and son slept, she composed a letter to an official who in the past had been stunned by her language abilities. Another time. A separate world. It took but a moment for her foot to rub it out.

IN ONE WAY THEY felt fortunate. The full viciousness of the Cultural Revolution toward intellectuals had missed them. If they had stayed in Beijing, they could have been murdered or been forced to suicide as the easy way out. But this exile had changed them physically. She was now a tiny husk of a woman, and he, an ancient praying mantis with homemade spectacles.

Every night now, she tried to walk off dreams. During the day, she daydreamed as she worked.

One evening she and he decided finally that daydreams are just that. They really had no way of getting their child out of this hellhole, as everything they could think of to expose his outstanding skills and genius to anyone here, or to try to contact someone in the outside world, would endanger him the more. The next morning, after their whispered conference, she was stopped on her way to the field by the collective's busiest busybody, the chief political officer, the woman with the keys, the human garbage that floated as garbage does, to the top, with a Party card to prove it.

"People have told me you are hurting their morale," said this defender of ideals. "It has been reported that your voice is not joyous during the weeding song. Please be joyous."

The next morning, this was found scratched on a freshly whitewashed wall of the People's Palace.

> *A pickled turnip in a bottle*
> *could sing 'The March of the Volunteers'*
> *but since no one looks in a bottle*
> *for a turnip who can sing*
> *the turnip was eaten.*

The poem was unsigned, but it was obvious to her husband and son who had penned it. Luckily, her history as a poet, and her skills, had been hidden from even the cadres on this farm. And since the majority of the work unit members were as unhappy in their private ways as she, the poem was quickly whitewashed out, but not before it was enjoyed and memorized by we'll never know how many. The sheer liberalism of it! By elevating the individual over the collective... Well, such a waste, this counterrevolutionary deviationist. Re-educated, that mind belonged in the Party's highest propaganda/arts unit.

More years passed as they both continued to educate Zhang Wenge as if, still unseen but approaching at speed, was his Shining Future.

ON THE SAME NIGHT in 1972 that Richard Nixon was toasting an absent Mao in the Great Hall of the People, and quoting the Chairman's poetry, the mother of eight-year-old Zhang Wenge took a walk to shake off her dreams, and happened to see the farm collective's pigs being fed and led by what smelt like *huangjiu*, cheap yellow liquor, the likes of which she'd never seen here. Without a single incriminating grunt, they were joining more besotted pigs to fill the back of a large anonymous truck. The whole silent, beautifully efficient action was being handled by three army officers. Three more were handling the transfer of a pile of bags and a number of drums to the Palace's office, supervised by a woman whose face was too indistinct in the darkness to make out, but one didn't need to see her face. As the 'Communism is Heaven' song goes,

> *The commune is the ladder.*
> *If we climb that ladder,*
> *We can climb the heights.*

Zhang's mother slipped closer without being seen.

Bags, of *rice!* Drums, of *cooking oil!* Two bags of *sugar!* Four cans of *ham!*

They were being loaded into the office... through that, to... no! The Armoury held all the munitions the collective might need, ready to defend against splittists, revisionists, any counterrevolutionary army. That backroom the cadres loved to talk about as the bulwark had always been more securely locked than even the grain store. Locked but at the ready, guarded by the cadres, ever vigilant.

The door was open now, and it was no armoury. It was a secret store, and the fat cadre supervising had the keys. And to think that just a year ago, the whole pig work unit had been trucked away for not shutting up the pigs, and for lying about it.

The woman who'd been stripped of her heroic name years ago and was now a dull shadow, ran out into the fields and then home without being seen, did a few things—and returned.

The cadre and all the army men were quietly joking together by the door, unfamiliar white twists of tobacco smoke rising from the group.

The back of the truck was filled with pigs, lumpenly lying in drunken sleep.

She slipped underneath and cut the fuel line.

She was undecided what to do next. Try to get to the farm's siren? Scream?

Stubs of cigarettes were being pocketed. Something had to be done.

She was just going to scream when she heard a strange sound. Singing. It was one of the new patriotic things they'd been taught. It had a good tune but who would want to waste their sleeplessness on that?

Are you new ghosts? she thought into the night. She'd learned that you don't have to speak to talk to ghosts.

But none of them answered.

The singing came closer, accompanied by the stamping beat of feet on the march.

From the corner of her eye, she saw the cadre lock the door to that Ali Baba's cave of a back room. The army men took up an official stance.

The singing changed its tone from measured to frenzied patriotism and joy. Then it all fell apart as a dozen teenagers came running into view.

These could be none other than the unwanted educated, in their teens and early twenties, all of whom should be starting out careers. They'd been shoved out from Shanghai, Beijing, all the cities, to 'learn from peasants' because the Party needed to disperse them, break up their power, shove the problem that there were no opportunities for them under the rug. They were no-choice 'volunteers' from the Up to the Mountains and Down to the Villages movement. How did she know all this? The cadres' excited reports about this wonderful new movement. She and her husband had deduced the rest.

She was so stunned by the scene that she wandered out into the open, between the loaded truck and the People's Palace. The group arrived, spread out according to their states of exhaustion. The flimsy city clothes they wore, the impractical shoes, the bundles they carried, all were astounding. And what was this girl and boy carrying that was so heavy? Two cases and a bundle wrapped in a quilt.

They dropped cases and bundle in front of her and stretched their fingers.

The bundle was unmistakable.

"Books?" she asked.

"Saved from university library!" said the girl.

"Don't let anyone see them."

"Don't worry, auntie," said the girl. "Once I teach you to read, they won't frighten you."

"Enough of that," said the boy. "We are here to learn from *you*. The educated learn from the peasants. Now we're hungry, so where's your canteen?"

'Auntie' smiled. "Now that's a question you could ask these army men stealing all our pigs, and that grasping capitalist cadre hiding food for herself and who else, in the back room *there*."

The boy goggled. This was all too much. The girl calmly said, "Let's all go say hello to the people in charge here. Boys, you know what to do?"

And the 'auntie' who was no auntie calmly accompanied the group of boys to the People's Palace, where the boys' enthusiasm overcame their lack of finesse in overpowering the startled army men, the cadre herself, and the other two Party hacks hiding close by.

'Auntie' was just going to crank up the alarm to have everyone come running as witnesses, when the boys broke down the door to the fake armoury, urged on by the girl.

The young people were so patriotic, so incensed at this corruption, one of them struck a match and threw it into the back room while others went to kill the pigs.

An exploding drum woke enough people that everyone came running.

'Auntie', the slip of a woman who had been that brave girl of the Long March, tried to save what she could, but a tongue of flame caught her.

THE FARM'S 'ARMOURY' WAS still exploding, drums of cooking oil shooting shrapnel and flames while bags of rice stunk frustratingly. One man ran around screaming, his skin on fire, having tried to grab a bag of rice. Burning oil and sticky rice grains made his skin a pitch-black sky pinpointed with glowing red stars. The smells. . .

And Zhang Dingtianlidi? Indomitable Spirit? Zhang Chen couldn't see her. He hoped she burned so fast and hot that she burned pure, and travelled straight to her destination, one where she would be provided for. There was indeed, enough for her to eat. Hell, there was enough for her to trade. To be a capitalist pig, if she so wished.

The smells... He hoped she wasn't part of them. They'd made his mouth water. Stuck memories up into his brain that crowded the horror, the stench of burnt rice, burnt flesh. Street-vendor temptations of hot oil and overtoasted sesame from the little *shao ping* hot-cakes, the long deepfried salty twists. Caramelised, sticky, skewered strips of pork.

He swallowed saliva, hating himself. But there was no time for that. *Think! Think, for her, for this moment.* It was the only way he could survive to do what he must, for her, for her. Ever since they'd arrived here, her heroic name stripped from her, he hadn't known what to think of her as to name. All he could think now was, "Dingtianlidi is dead." No *Long may she 'live'.* For all her attempts to tell him *there is another stage beyond this one*, he couldn't truly believe.

His son reached for his hand, pulling him home.

Zhang Chen wanted to throw himself into the collective's well. But there was his son to think of.

Home, there were two raw sweet potatoes that he shoved in his son's pockets. He grabbed the cold porridge pot and wrapped it in a bundle, dug up his stones and pocketed them. His son had made up a bundle of things for them and was waiting to take his hand. They fled as the walls of the Palace fell in among themselves from the effects of fire and the bashing down by members of the work unit beating back everything including each other and the new volunteers, to get at what they could.

Father and son had only gone a little ways off when they heard a shot.

They didn't stop running till they had reached an area so rocky and pitted, they had to be very careful, and no one would want to follow. An hour later they reached a dark, wild forest, the kind most peasants would keep well out of because of all the ghosts.

"We'll stop here."

Zhang Chen lifted the lid of the pot. No sorghum porridge. She'd scrubbed it clean. But it wasn't empty. A fat jade-green and gold cabbage caterpillar and one cabbage leaf outshone the forest's gloom. And under the leaf, a small roll the size of a cocoon—tied with a strand of caterpillar silk. The roll opened up to be a strip of thin but tough paper, the stuff given out to write self-denunciations.

> *Beloved,*
> *Remember what the lowliest caterpillar achieves without a Plan.*
> *Know that you never have to avert your face again.*
> *I watch you when you sleep as you did, me.*
> *Perpetual immortality!*
> *Fly, butterfly*
> *with our son on your back*
> *carrying your stones.*
> *Cook this in your rice to feed you both*
> *and go.*

He who had always scoffed at ghosts and tolerated with good cheer but barely put up with all that immortality poetry she had once written, did as he was told. He wouldn't have known what to do with the caterpillar before. If anyone on the farm had seen him put it on that cabbage leaf... well, those days were gone.

Three nights later, under a full moon, he took his son's hand and set off for his second long march. He had no money but he had those stones. He only had to trade a few, for what stones don't have special powers if you need them and there is no available cure? His homemade spectacles didn't hurt, either. *It's impossible to truly drive out superstition*, he decided, when he saw how much awe he instilled without opening his mouth. Perhaps the effect was aided by those four white hairs that had sprouted from his chin. As for permits and danger, the chaos of the Cultural Revolution, and the aftermath of the Vietnam War actually made their travels easier. His plan, which developed from listening to people on the road, was to go through Vietnam, and out to Australia on a boat.

They were almost to the border of Vietnam when a fluke of someone recognizing him turned into his arrest. He and his son were fed, formally identified, and then he was interviewed in a such a confusingly respectful manner, he demanded to hold his son's hand, lest the child be taken away. If they were to be shot or dumped in a well, the pain and fright to the boy would be so much shorter if they were killed together.

Instead, they were rushed off to a military transport, and flown back to the very same institute in Beijing that he'd been torn from in the aftermath of the famine (which was now named 'the Difficult Three-Year Period').

The Institute, like so many seats of higher learning that had been infested, had been culturally cleaned so thoroughly, its halls still echoed. He was not only made Director of a new department, with instructions to find more staff, but his son was now treated as a 'natural red', a child of a high-ranking cadre.

Once Zhang Chen saw and solved his main problem fitting into the new culture, he and his son did fine. On the collective farm, *moyanggong*, pretending to work, had been a serious offence. At the Institute, it was expected of someone at his position.

THAT CATERPILLAR WAS A triumph. It ate voraciously in the house they'd made for it—a large square-sided glass jar with beamed ceiling of latticed bamboo. One day, it ate nothing. Instead, it inched up and along, pulled a silk rope from its bottom and hung itself. As they watched, it dangled, turning, wrapping, till it was hidden in its own cocoon, where it performed its next magic trick—metamorphosis into pupa, creating its next most spectacular magic trick of all.

Luckily for father and son, the magic trick was performed as if waiting for their attendance.

Zhang Wenge saw the curtains open—the pupa begin to split. "Forget about your tea," he called. "It's begun."

Zhang Chen's eyes were wet when it was over.

His son exploded in laughter.

"You've been keeping this a secret!" he said. "Such an anticlimax."

The butterfly was such an ugly little nondescript, quite unlike the gorgeous creature of its young life. A peasant of a butterfly. They opened the window but it flew to the edge of a cup of sugared tea. They fed it this butterfly's wine and melon juice and honey-water and left the window open but it liked being indoors until one morning when it went out briefly, then came back in, flitting around the small flat, where they lost track of it, and only found it later, a sooty smudge by a chair's leg.

UNDER ZHANG CHEN'S WISE leadership (in which he hid as much as possible, his intellectual curiosity and interest in actual agricultural reform while promoting both) his department developed innovative pest control measures, excelling with earworm in maize. He also became quietly known abroad for his startling findings on the codling moth.

In 1987, shortly after he retired, Zhang Chen had an exhibition in a little room upstairs in that huge Beijing temple built with a vaulted ceiling so that the Dongfeng 1 guided missile points heavenwards—the Military Museum of the Chinese People's Revolution.

Twelve small stones were displayed, each covered with water in its own common blue and white sesame-seed pattern rice bowl. Zhang Chen sat by the door, this little husk of man, curled on a tubular-metal chair. His deeply lined face rose when anyone made it up past the tanks, missiles and dioramas of glorious victories, to this quiet little cell. His ears weren't tuned to the comments of the few visitors, or he would have heard:

"My father was on the Long March, too."

"Oh, sure he was. Pull the other one. I bet he'd been a landlord."

"It's so unfair. Look at that old guy. Who's interested in his silly rocks? He only gets this because he's always had a cushy life, being pals with Mao back then. They get free train travel and a nurse, you know."

"Hahah!"

"No, it's true."

The free train travel with a registered nurse for the venerable veterans of the Long March *was* true.

One thing he'd forgotten about in his years of urban exile was the thick air of Beijing—the coal smoke that settled in the wide dusty city bowl, especially on winter nights. On the collective farm out in the back of beyond, winds would whisk the sky cleaner than he'd appreciated. From his first winter as a restored Party member, working at the pace of a favoured citizen in coddled, comfortable surroundings, he spent each winter trying and failing to keep from breathing the poisoned smoke; as impossible as sifting air.

Each winter a raw throat would arrive first, followed before the day was out with a cough bristling with blades, then great gobs of phlegm coloured by someone with a sense of humour. People's-Liberation-Army-green slime filled his lungs, throat, tracheal tubes, even the secret backrooms of his ears. Each winter siege was followed by the spring retreat, till the year he retired, the year his son started university.

Spring saw him completely blocked with phlegm, shutting off all sound. In the progressive hospital, he was told he had 'sticky ear', that it would clear up on its own accord, or not; neither modern nor traditional remedies would work. That was true. By late summer when flame-red persimmons were piled on plates at Party banquets, he was declared profoundly deaf, and offered hearing aids.

He gratefully took up the offer. They were heavy and caught on his spectacles. They helped him to hear sounds from the real world. But most importantly, they helped to drown out the other.

His profound deafness had created a void, an opportunity. *Nature abhors a vacuum.* As a man experienced with the evils of the social good, he could have expected what would happen, but still, he wasn't prepared when it did.

'Red Tide' sung by a crowd of 10,000—he could hear himself in the middle of it, his lungs bursting with song. The two minutes of the song he'd loved the most, on a loop. The song loops never stopped, though they would change. Sometimes he could hear his son also as they were surrounded by the hoarse strains of fellow Party banqueteers, their throats burnt raw from *shaojiu* toasts at the most dangerous camaraderie-fest of all, the *jiu xi*, the drinking banquet. Worst was a verse from 'March of the Volunteers' with a low drone just perceptible—his wife sounding like she had in the early days of their love. She never talked loud enough for him to hear, always being, when he almost understood, drowned out by the shouting singers, the loudest of whom was always him.

All the sounds—songs and words—were real, said his brain. They'd taken over, and even with the aid of the hearing device, showed themselves more vigorous than the filmy and unsubstantial real world sounds.

His wife's voice was so real, so real he could almost smell her breath. And she started to come to him in dreams, not as she had died, but as the beautiful young heroine, Dingtianlidi.

Without hardly mentioning it to his son, now busy with his university studies, he took up that Long Marcher privilege of train travel with nurse, and spent a month going back to the back of beyond, where he both charmed and alarmed her by jumping out and digging in the strangest places. He built up another collection of stones holding miniature worlds, planning to give them to his son.

The nurse found the stones fascinating, and not only that, was uncommonly kind and caring to the old man. She called him 'Grandfather', loved to ply him with little treats—chicken leg with foot on a stick, a fancy package of pickled mustard greens. She was always making him tea, and made the train crew share with him the dumplings she caught them making for themselves. She was the greatest nuisance he'd ever known, but he shed his distrust of others enough to call her 'little dove' and mean it. She was so unscientifically minded that he wondered how she'd passed her course. Whereas he had only thought of taking this trip as a diversion from his hauntings, thinking that doing something might banish them, she really did believe there were worlds the stones had trapped.

By the time the trip was over, he believed her. After all, how could he prove her wrong, when the 'real' world was at the mercy of a battery?

He decided to give his son the stones—to open his eyes to the *real* real world. But on arriving home, seeing Zhang Wenge's bowed back and haggard face—the boy was studying so much in preparation (or maybe escape from me?), he thought "What good will it do him?" and said nothing.

The exhibition of stones was arranged by, of all people, the nurse, whose uncle... Connections! The nurse had told the uncle, "That empty room at the museum you complain about. You can have something special. A display by a real veteran—something that brings the struggle to the youth in such human terms, more than just the hardware downstairs." *She's sharp*, thought the uncle, who had her reassigned to a propaganda unit, where she was very unhappy.

The display was Zhang Chen. The stones were irrelevant.

"What's the *use* of him?" said a visitor, "All these old ones we're supposed to support."

"Yeah, but I wish I'd met Mao."

"Hnh."

"This is boring. I know where to find a bottle of Coke."

Some visitors who had chuckled at first at the amateurish display, surprised themselves by being hooked. Each water-rounded stone encased an almost hidden world straight out of the Chinese paintings where towering rocks shoot straight up from the paddies and twisted trees hang on by their toenails as a tiny ox and driver approach on a hair's-breadth winding road. The people who stayed the longest, shoving their faces down into the glass cases to see more detail, were invariably international tourists who couldn't read Chinese and therefore thought the old man in the chair an indigent who'd nabbed a sheltered spot to sleep. They expected that once a guard noticed, the vagrant be chucked out.

The last day of the exhibition was very quiet. A few flies buzzed in the spring dust as Zhang Chen curled more and more into himself in his chair. After closing, a guard found him. He looked like a typically grotesque insect moult, all life flown, but attached to his small bare head, a pair of comic spectacles hanging on.

Zhang Wenge wasn't surprised. In fact, he was happy for his father, and a small untended corner of him was hopeful. The old man had become increasingly difficult. He'd take off his hearing aids and invite his son to "really *listen*. Listen past what you hear". He told his son that the stones really do hold worlds. He even, quite alarmingly in the last few days of his life, talked about that nurse. "I should get her to meet you so you can both escape together." It was so much better that he died as he did, hoping his ridiculous, dangerous thoughts.

Zhang Wenge immediately put into action his father's wishes. Zhang Chen's dearest wish, uncharacteristically disobeyed, was that his son escape while he, the father, was still alive, damn the consequences. Zhang Chen didn't care that the Party would strip him of everything. How rich he would be. A fillip to that hallowed Cultural Revolution slogan *Better to be poor under socialism than rich under capitalism.* Zhang Chen's second dearest wish was that his son strip himself of the Cultural Revolution itself, changing his Wenge to, say, Arthur, and that he'd live somewhere as Arthur Zhang.

ARTHUR ZHANG ARRIVED IN Sydney as a student in January 1989. He carried with him the one stone his father had asked him to keep, and some of the hopes of his father as well as his own more modest expectations.

Within a month he was jilted of his education fees by one of the many dodgy fake degree factories taking advantage of Australia's international education business. He had two degrees already, the first in Chinese literature and the second, in entomology, both deemed useless as far as Australia's migration wonts went. Chinese literature was a no-brainer. Entomologists, as with all science-degreed people in Australia, were fighting each other for the few jobs on offer. To give a position to someone who couldn't say 'r', was laughable, he was told in an interview in which his papers had been looked at, exclusively. He never got a chance to talk. Arthur could not only speak English, but he spoke with a careful fluency. His father had urged him to learn secretly from listening to smuggled tapes, and to change his name to something with an 'r' in it as soon as he landed in some promised land.

Fat lot of good this got me, he said to himself. He had lost his money in this expensive city, was liable to have his visa revoked, couldn't get a job in this country where he was more educated than most— both in high culture and hard science. He would have been faced with two choices—leave or hide—but with no money he could only hide. He was staring at bushes in the park by Central Station when a young man sat next to him on the bench.

"Speak English?"

"And Mandarin and Cantonese. Can you?"

"Hey, man, back off. Your clothes and all that."

"I am sorry. It's been—"

"None taken. I bet you want to throw a brick through a window or two."

Arthur laughed a little, as he expected he should. He didn't know how to identify Australian secret police.

"Dude," the guy said. "If you're scoping out the bushes, they're full occupancy." Arthur hadn't heard English used this way, but he caught the gist, and figured the young man for what Arthur had heard described as an ABC—Australian-born Chinese. Most likely a young, privileged university student no older than eighteen.

There were indeed a lot of ragged men and women with all their possessions, like those illegals from the countryside people looked away from in Beijing.

"I rather guessed," said Arthur.

"If you wait here a mo, I can get you picked up and taken to a little place in western Sydney where there's as much work as you want, and no worries. A market garden—bok choy and all that. You know bok choy." He smiled apologetically, "Shit pay, but lodging in a shed. Very private."

Arthur, already twenty-five years old, remembered, in spite of all the horrors at the farm, how much he had liked to dig in the soil, care for growing plants. Had loved the buzz of supposed pests.

He readily accepted, was transported to the place safely and with no drama—and there he worked, slept, ate, worked, talked to pretty much no one, lived such a quiet life that he felt as if he had hung himself, wrapped in a cocoon of his own making... or had he just hung himself?

Months passed. Momentous changes in the world. Neither that student nor his family told Arthur. They didn't want to lose him. He learned the news from the used *Herald*s and *Telegraph*s he picked up each night at the local bus-stop bin.

First, the horrors of Tiananmen Square. He was illegal in Australia, but could never go back.

His mother and father came to him in dreams, father telling him to use the stones if he had to, to bribe his way to safety; mother asking if he could trust these people who knew where he was. Arthur always woke thinking, *Pathetic! Having to create dreams to have anyone care about you.* He was always ready to run, but he was trapped.

Then one night he opened up the paper to read that Prime Minister Bob Hawke had just emotionally declared an amnesty for immigrants. Specifically, thousands of mainland Chinese who'd come to Australia to study!

WITH A LOAN FROM the family he worked for, at tough but honest terms, he purchased their plot, their farting old truck—and a five minute drive away in the nearest neighbourhood, a practically comatose small fruit and veg shop two blocks away from a sparkling new Westfield Mall. He named the shop *Zhang's Infinite Immortals Fruit and Veg*, thinking of a poem by his mother.

> *To be fresh is to be young.*
> *Who wants to be young*
> *when you can be experienced?*
>
> *Infinite immortals are the sheen that disappears when dry,*
> *are the body and shiftiness of smoke,*
> *Sit still, the young are told,*
> *while the old sit jammed in by immortals' buttocks.*
> *Gaining wisdom? More likely, arthritis.*

*Better to steep in a bath, which no immortal will stick a
toe in.*
Still, you can be young and not be fresh.
*A New Year's mandarin orange sitting on the shelf
quickly grows a furry blue, wet bottom.*

When he was four or five, he once asked his
mother, "Where does Time go?" His father would
have been angry at such a nonsense question. His
mother said, "Round and round."

PRACTICALLY AT THE SAME spot on the Great
Cosmic circle that Arthur was, on the very day that
Arthur opened his Immortals, Melmet Bulgurluoğlu
exploded.

"Bıktım!" She clapped a hand over her mouth.

"They're at school," said her husband, nuzzling her
neck as he wrapped his arms around her waist.
"What's wrong?"

She twisted out of his grasp, wiping away a tear.

"Just *look* at these, Bülent. They're covered in
bedsores." She'd flipped a whole tray of purple
eggplants over, each eggplant fat and shiny as a whale
on top, its underside a gory, oozing mess.

"And these zucchinis!" She picked one up and wagged it in his face. "What is this, the fifth produce supplier we've had?"

Bülent sighed. She was so right. Didn't any of them have any pride?

"I'll try another," he said, scratching his head.

"You won't find one there. What about this Mr Zhang next door? He's just opened. I tested him with a kilo of pears and he tossed one away rather than put it in my bag. Even *I* couldn't see what was wrong with it.

"I can't do that, my dear fig. He's not a wholesaler. He's probably never done wholesale."

"I never made a *tulumba tatlisi* until I did." Her forehead wrinkled as she wiped eggplant-bedsore goo off her fingers onto the white cloth folded around her waist.

O, Melmet, thought her husband. *Your logic is unique.*

Bülent mentally flexed his mind to get ready to approach this Mr Zhang he'd never met, hadn't noticed, his life being entirely his family and Ali Baba's. He *so* hated feeling like a fool, and he so often did. *Tomorrow*, he promised himself. *Sometime soon, I promise*. He wanted so much to run away from the ridiculous job. He wished he could lie to his wife, saying he'd asked and of course, a retail fruiterer has to buy from wholesalers just as any restaurant does.

Bülent's moustache twitched as he thought back to a scene when they had just moved into the tiny flat above the restaurant and were still cleaning up the mess left by the previous owners of what had been the kind of 'restaurant' that serves reheated fish and chips and some other fried horror called a chiko roll. Bülent had just sketched out for her on a scrap of paper what he was going to get a sign maker to do. He was a good letterer, and the design was beautiful.

"But Bülent, my cedar," she said gently, putting her hand on his. "Why Akçabaat?"

"How can it be anything but? We come from there." He pulled his hand away as if she'd stung him. "Are you ashamed?"

"Course no! But Aussies." She pointed to the 'ç'. "They look at that, think 'apple with worm'. And how does they say it? How does they say, Let go to . . *auk, ak.* . . So they say, 'We go Thai.'"

"Ceviz kabugunda firtina."

"Not in front of the children!"

Sami, their first, was busy gumming one of her baby-sized homemade teething rings, a salty *susamli simit* sesame biscuit, while their second child was listening from her womb.

She was right. They couldn't burden the children. He hung his head. "Storm in a walnut shell," he said, feeling especially bad because learning English was so much harder for her whose work was never done. It hadn't occurred to him, but she insisted she was *not* going to have the children start school being foreign speakers.

"Do you have a name for the restaurant?" he asked.

"Ali Baba."

"Ali Baba! Every Turkish restaurant outside Turkey is named Ali Baba."

Her unpruned eyebrow lifted with beautiful eloquence.

She was always right. And she could cook like nobody else, *and* she had a belly more beautiful than a melon, and such delicious toes...

"Bülent, are you ignoring me purposely, or are you hibernating?"

He shook his pelt. "Of course not. Did you say something?"

"Only for the past five minutes. Before you do anything else, could you *please* make that sign I asked for, and install it before the staff comes today. You make such pretty signs, and you've left this so long, it's an emergency."

"Do you want a painted sign, or would you prefer a blackboard?"

"Not the menu! I told you, Bülent. If you don't want stones in our rice, then a big 'Do *not* pour boiling water down this sink.' Right *there*. I tell every worker but I might as well be pouring water through their ears. And they're as deaf to her screams as you are."

This was a bit of a sore spot. "I told you, heart of my desire, the screams are pipe expansion. There can't be a djinni in the drain. There *are* *no* djinn in Australia."

"Maybe there *were* *no*. But there were no *Bulgurluoğlus* here, either."

What can you say to that? She wasn't even arguing. She never argued. Always so logical, she just presented facts. He felt sheepish that she had to go to the trouble.

"I'll get straight onto it." He shambled off, chewing his moustache.

ARTHUR ZHANG SUPPOSED THAT his life in Australia was going well enough. He worked his bum off, being a productive market gardener as well as being surprisingly good at the fruit/veg biz. His shop looked colourful and cheery due to his love of colours, textures, shapes.

He bought a cheap computer and set it up in his beyond-dingy flat above the shop. And from there, he campaigned with a diligence that was admirable. It just wasn't credible that his scientific knowledge, experience, and practical skills were not needed by any scientific institution, university, agricultural or environmental business in Australia. It was unbelievable that, with all this stuff about Australia being part of Asia, and Australia being into high culture, his expertise in Chinese literature and culture was equally unvalued. *Unwanted* at universities, NGOs, trade associations, museums, even *Alliance Chinoise* (just kidding).

Every evening he took companions to bed, sometimes two or three. He'd wake with them poking him in the ribs, his warmth bringing out their stale perfumes of musky mildew. One night he wrote a poem about the homeless life of a library book. It was either pretty good or very bad in both Chinese and

English. Sometimes he recited his mother's poems back to himself and allowed himself to be objective. "Don't peel a poem," she once said. "But if you have to, write it in Russian."

In his dingy flat of minimalist fruit-box furniture he'd hacked together, and pillars of books, he became fascinated with objects of art, the more useless the better. Pierced-work vases and dishes, glazes meant to crack, translucent porcelains, landscapes painted on grains of rice, the search and arguments over the most exquisite shade and translucency of celadon green.

He gave a lecture at the local library. *Celadon Green: What is it and why is it important?* The librarians were chuffed to host this Fine Arts event, so very North Shore. For some reason, they scheduled it at 2 o'clock to 3, on a Tuesday, so he had to put up a Sorry for the Inconvenience notice and close the shop from 1 to 4, leaving time for questions. Eight people attended—all well-past their paid working years. Three of the people had been 'into pottery', two ladies knitted the whole time, and a retired professor came wanting to interrupt and then, after the talk was over, argue for fun. The head librarian finally intruded, helping the helpless Zhang. "That was fabulous," she said. "Much better than we expected. Would you like to give another talk next month?"

He discarded his thoughts of getting up in the informal intelligentsia that way, and continued to apply for jobs, month after month, year piling upon year.

Social life? He did go on one date. One of the Thursday night librarians smiled at him so persistently that he shyly asked her about a book he hadn't read but thought he should. They didn't have it and couldn't get it. "But," she said, "Have you seen the latest Star Wars?"

"No."

"Well, you should. I haven't seen it either. It's at the Odeon."

So this is how dating is done, he thought, hoping he didn't fall at the next step. "Would you like to go?"

First, they had dinner at a little Thai place she suggested. He was so keen to do the right thing that he went to the back and paid while she was still eating, before she opened the menu again and ordered dessert, a sticky-rice pudding that had looked repulsively stale when he saw it while waiting to pay. So she ate the pudding by herself making defensive jokes about her weight until he picked up the cue and told her how slim and attractive she was. She was clearly waiting for something more. He said he didn't like sweet foods, remembering too late that he'd just shared the sugar cane prawns. Even more stressful was his attempt to be good company, fun and witty. He'd last done it in those grotesque banquets blessedly long ago. All this was such a strain that he had trouble remembering that she was, objectively considered, attractive and not uneducated. Then he forgot to pay for her dessert and her other drink, and that was another mess.

The film was excruciating, but he thought *maybe the film doesn't matter, in which case wouldn't it be cheaper and more comfortable to sit on a park bench?* She talked through the whole thing while eating a progression of noisy snacks, but so was everyone else. Afterwards, as they strolled down block after block, looking for what she called 'something that takes our fancy' she took his arm. "The earlier Star Wars flicks were so much better, of course. But I still just *love* Yoda. Don't you just love him?"

"The popularity of elitism still underwhelms me."

"Whoa! Just who's the bloody elitist?"

As he strolled home, the terrible meal kept trying to come back up into his mouth, but it failed to dampen his mood. He was headily elated to be alone again.

"What the fuck was *I* about," he said to the spring night, the first time he experimented with 'fuck'. It sounded quite correct, appropriate to the circumstance. He regretted most that he'd have to change his library times. As for giving her his assessment of the movie—like putting a celadon porcelain plate under a Whopper. This was the second Star Wars movie he'd seen, and it hadn't converted him. Yoda in particular made him see red, made him almost anti-Western. To show true Wisdom, dress someone in some quasi Eastern getup and have him spout ridiculous simplisms made profound by ridiculous grammar, grammar that would condemn an immigrant as ignorant.

Yes, the wisdom of Stars Wars works for the masses here, because it is 'entertainment'—so superficial, yet believed without question. The ridiculousness made him feel quite angry. Alienated. Alien.

But *hey, as they'd say here. Don't be too heavy. The West hasn't yet discovered, beyond '7' and '30 days', the wisdom and power of numbers, specifically the list whose title has strength because of the number, such as the Three Antis, or the hedging one's bets with numbers One Attack and Three Against*

*Campaign. Turn any inanity into a Four or Five Something—
even the dizzy Four-Facing Policy—and you've got the power to
kill millions,* without the expense of building anything,
let alone a Death Star. *Still, I shouldn't be so hard on silly
Western entertainment. Give me Star Wars any day, over
Cultural Revolution Opera.* By this time he was back in
bed with three companions. When he woke the next
morning, granted, one of them had left bruises, but
none of them had irritated him.

He had such a lone existence. Almost no contact
with the world outside his mind.

Of course, there were the Bulgurluoğlus—Melmet,
her husband Bülent, and their children who were
growing up faster than weeds grow. But that had been
a brief flirtation, years ago already.

ARTHUR ZHANG THOUGHT BACK to the first day he
met Bülent Bulgurluoğlu, maybe a month after Arthur
put up the banner he'd calligraphed himself, 'Grand
opening', and hung his beautifully painted sign *Zhang's
Infinite Immortals Fruit and Veg.* The big shaggy man
with a comically sheepish look walked into the
Immortals just after a rush of customers. He was

balancing on one arm, an enormous platter covered with a spotless white cloth.

"I'm from Ali Baba's," he said, "the restaurant next door." He stuck out an unbelievably huge hand. "Bülent Bulgurluoğlu. Bülent. Or in Aussie, just call me Bull Ant. My wife, Melmet. She thought you'd like—" He looked around but there wasn't a flat place large enough.

"Arthur," said Arthur, putting his wiry hand into Bülent's, who didn't shake it but clasped it over-gently. *A reformed hand-crusher?*

"Thank you very much, Bülent," said Arthur, taking the loaded tray. "Would you and uh, Melmet, like this with tea?" Before he reached 'tea', up his neck rose a fire that reached his cheeks.

Bülent Bulgurluoğlu threw up his hands and clapped them, smiling broadly "She's always doing things like this. I thought *I'd* be the embarrassed one." He took the tray from Arthur and slipped smoothly back of the shop, where he laid it on an emptied fruit box.

He waited there while Arthur served a new glut of customers.

When they left, he returned. "My wife, Melmet, you see." He shuffled uncomfortably. "She thought you might be able to supply our produce. I know we should just find another wholesaler. So don't worry about saying no. I understand, but possibly anyway, no offence, Arthur. Do you know of anyone who sells cabbages and such that haven't been poisoned? Frankly, I like holes in my cabbages, and the odd grub."

He blurted it all out so awkwardly that Arthur Zhang saw instantly why this man had such a loving and delectable wife. For Arthur remembered her from few weeks ago, when she came in saying her husband liked pears. She smelled like an exotic perfume, a mix of a number of scents that often wandered over from next door. He'd wanted to go there as a customer, but had worried that they'd recognize him and not charge him. And he'd wanted to go over with a basket of lovely fruits and vegetables, but he hadn't because the fruit and veg he sold in the shop was the highest quality he could source commercially, but compared to his garden plot, was utter trash, to his taste. So he didn't give them anything and felt increasingly awkward. He'd been ashamed not to *give* the nice woman, Bülent's wife, the pears, and ashamed that they weren't the celestial quality she deserved for— now that he'd met Bülent—her loving husband.

O, how awkwardness can be the oil that allows friendship to slip into stone exteriors.

That night when the restaurant closed, Arthur was waiting. He led Bülent Bulgurluoğlu through the dark shop into the backroom behind the backroom, to his secret stash. Cabbages were lacy with fattening caterpillars. There were so many sleeping butterflies in the place that it reminded Bulgurluoğlu of his sister-in-law's house, ever since she'd been widowed. But this was so much better. Fifteen butterflies in a room, even when active, must be a joy. Butterflies neither use litterboxes, nor do their feet shred chairs. Arthur Zhang's private room had plants growing everywhere as well as harvested produce, "all from my own little plot" said Arthur, "but don't tell."

They admired everything together, the smell and taste, and the wildlife. The carved-out bits of eggplants only added to their charm, the apples with personality had, perhaps, a happy inhabitant that Bülent searched for with a thick but tender finger.

Arthur Zhang never thought he'd show his treasures to anyone, but he couldn't help himself. He pulled off a cabbage leaf and spread it on the table.

Bülent Bulgurluoğlu bent over it, his thick eyebrows hiding his face, but his shoulders and back said enough.

"It's so Turkish," said Bulgurluoğlu.

"It's so Chinese. Those swirls and scallops. Those incredibly detailed cutouts. Those colours. The *writing*."

"Exactly."

Arthur was almost angry, but at the same time he was so charmed and surprised.

He pulled the Turkish/Chinese/Turkish artpiece out from under Bülent and plonked in its place, a large glass jar just like those Melmet displayed in Ali Baba's, filled with her scrumptious purple turnip pickles. This one was loosely filled with nasturtium leaves and capped with a rubber-banded cloth. The inside of the glass had been worked with an abstract design of silvery lines.

"Put your ear to it," said Arthur.

Bülent did, and heard his blood flooshing back and forth.

"It's not easy," said Arthur. "Relax. Take your hand away from your other ear."

". . . Oh!" Bülent cocked his head up at Arthur and went back to listening. "It's surprisingly loud."

"They don't eat with their mouth closed. Snails. They have sharp teeth."

Bulgurluoğlu's smile was so huge, his teeth peeked out from under that enormous broom. "Their crunching makes me hungry for nasturtiums."

"Excuse me," said Arthur. "I think someone's at the door."

Bülent cried out something unintelligible and slapped his head with both hands. "I've left Melmet and the children all evening."

Melmet was at the roller door, grinning like a mischievous cat. She was holding the hands of two sleepy children—Sami in Batman pajamas, and his younger sister Hurrem in a bees and blossoms nightie. Melmet's apologies for disturbing were almost drowned in Bülent's embrace of the three of them at once.

"This is Arthur," he said, turning, his arms filled with children. "Arthur, I am sorry. Sleeptime cannot happen without storytime."

The next day, Arthur forgave Bülent's ignorance of Chinese art enough that he delivered a large heavy square that he'd wrapped in butcher paper. It went up on the wall of the restaurant within the hour, taking the place of the picture of Topkapi. This cabbage leaf that he'd trimmed the stem off—perfectly preserved in all its brilliant and subtle colours, sharp lines and delicate tracery—made Melmet put her hands to her face, she was so overcome. She ordered Bülent never to tell the children nor any customers what it really was.

Bülent kept his lips sealed, but that framed piece of work got a reputation all its own, scholars drifting into Ali Baba's, some ordering distractedly, some not even making the pretence of being a customer—and all, having left to return to their towers, arguing about its provenance. One school of thought—nay, certainty— spawned a number of fakes when the piece was declared the lost-for-centuries subterfuginous, secretly coded work of the great Turkish calligraphy master, the eunuch Yaqut al-Mustasimi, scribe to the last caliph of Baghdad.

Bülent and Melmet were so busy that day and evening that it was close to midnight already when Bülent was able to visit Arthur Zhang again. Melmet had arranged it with Arthur, visiting him for a moment during the day. From what she had gathered from her husband, the two men had, as the Aussie saying goes, 'got on like a house on fire'. She was delighted for them, even though Bülent was his usual scattered self. He and Mr Zhang had chattered like birds and like birds, never got around to business.

So at just past midnight, after Bülent had delivered yet another gargantuan platter of ambrosial delights, he and Arthur made the deal. Arthur would provide all the produce for Ali Baba's, as much as possible from his garden plot. The restaurant would return all lodgers and artists to Arthur. The first delivery: tomorrow morning, 8:45 sharp.

COME NEXT MORNING, ARTHUR made his first delivery at 8:41, laying on the top of the pile of baskets and boxes a bouquet of sweet-pea flowers. Bülent had kept the details a surprise, so he watched Melmet unpack with glee and pride.

She was besotted with the freshness, the scents, the gorgeous skin textures, complexions, the complex tastes, and all the special care Arthur had gone to in selecting the beauteous bounty he delivered, but. *O, Bülent! It's a blessing, and a curse, that you see only what your heart sees.*

You can't convince most people that the healthy caterpillar munching on your salad is a guarantee of quality. And whatever staff they got, and good staff was so hard to find, they weren't about to comb through what Melmet knew they'd call a 'bunch of wormy garbage'.

"Aussies," she said, holding up a finely engraved zucchini. "What do they know of taste? Garden? Inspectors, Bülent! They'll shut us down. Lawyers. Perhaps our citizenship. Police. . . "

So the arrangement changed. The restaurant got all the regular stuff, the commercial kind people bought from the fruit and veg. He selected the best he could, of course, as he always did. And he charged Ali Baba's cost plus petrol. He refused to take any more than that; the Bulgurluoğlus were not only neighbours, but that odd thing he'd only heard of but never had before—friends. The exclusives from Arthur's plot were shared between him and Melmet and Bülent and his charges in the plot itself and his 'petting farm in the back-of-beyond room' (as the children, when older, dubbed that craziness). They wouldn't touch the stuff.

And these next-door-neighbour friends each prospered in their own way.

ZHANG'S IMMORTALS DID WELL, though you mightn't know it. His clothes were always clean but only worn for function. His plot gave him quiet joy, and he also gained both pleasure and pride from the glee which attended his constant gifts to the Bulgurluoğlus. Not the kids, mind you. But Melmet especially, crooned over the fresh chickpeas he grew for her. The cabbage rolls she made from his 'balls of lace' as she called them were too good for mere mortals, Bülent swore. She loved picking out and returning what she called 'your gourmet diners'. And she loved her husband having such a dear dear friend. "So un-Aussie mate," she liked to say. She loved bringing over a pot of her delicious apple tea for them.

Both she and her husband were so touchy. Their whole family was. Arthur found it disconcerting at first, all the spontaneous bear-hugs. The violent way Bülent's arms would suddenly spring straight forward to grasp your shoulders and pull you in for a quick kiss to both cheeks. The only physical manifestation of love that he'd ever known in his family was a look. It was a picture worth a thousand words and all, but. . .

But. Sometimes a word in one language and one tone, can never come across to another language with its soul intact. Around the friendship with the Bulgurluoğlus, there grew an insurmountable *But.* Like some hedges, it was so slow-growing that no one saw it till it was already too high to climb over. The Bulgurluoğlu children's needs, Ali Baba's needs including innovations like the installation of the *nargile* area, 'Hookah corner', to get younger customers in the evening. Today's needs, tomorrow's needs. . .

The relationship became so strained that Arthur took to making his deliveries like a very dependable ghost, and Melmet would pick them up and pay him the same way, slipping an envelope through his back door. They were both relieved not to see each other.

Bülent was especially embarrassed to see Arthur. He had loved being with the man, had thought him a kind of Chinese *khoja*, a wise man, not that he'd told Arthur. Bülent hated how he'd been with Arthur. He felt dirtily guilty for opening his mouth, which had taken advantage of Arthur's talents, knowledge and selfless kindness. All that shopping Zhang had done for the Bulgurluoğlus over the years, each of Arthur's careful deliveries, his gifts from his magical garden that he'd taken to delivering in sealed plastic bags—all that from this extraordinary, love-deprived man. Sometimes Bülent wanted to cry, sometimes to crush the man to his chest, but he made sure to not get anywhere near him. He felt so lucky, so blessed, that he didn't want to dirty the man. Or maybe, Bülent said to himself, you're just a coward.

Whatever Arthur felt, they avoided each other as Zhang's Immortals, Ali Baba's, and the children thrived.

MEANWHILE... ARTHUR MUSED ABOUT its meaning. Thinking back to his mother's poems, it occurred to him that if she had been a poet in the English language, she would have loved that word. It says so much about one's place. Here he was, a *meanwhile* on the circle, like a speck of dust that hadn't been cleaned, while the circle itself shimmered with activity whizzing round and round its depths.

He kept applying for positions till he embarrassed himself by being remembered at some university as a loser, uh, 'having applied before'. He'd read about the need for tutors, so he went to the local newspaper to advertise.

A man there with the eyes of a rooster who's seen too many neck-wringings, was kind enough, after a little chat when he asked Arthur some very odd questions, to tell him not to bother. "'Single man, no teaching qualifications, wants to teach your children.' It doesn't wash," he said. "Although you could get more jobs than you could handle, if you're into no-contact work—homework and papers. I could link you up. Parents are too time-poor to do their children's homework now."

"Thank you for your help," said Arthur.

"You're not interested?"

"I don't mean to offend you, but what you've told me makes me sad."

Those tragic eyes crinkled. "It makes me fucken, excuse my French, *furious*."

THE CIRCLE GLEAMS AS years slip along it like someone else's sentimental charms.

ARTHUR KEPT UP HIS learning, which was ridiculously easy. Genes, he reckoned. Languages came so easily that he invented projects to track histories of syntax, word forms, curses, idioms. At times, he experienced great, visceral thrills of discovery, only to waste more time thinking of how important, how meaningful these were. He'd then please Futility by writing papers that piled up. He had to write them, but at least he had enough pride to save them from exposure and rejection. One day he made himself put his most important discovery into words, for his education: *I'm an explorer but say I discover something. A nobody can't discover something, for even discovery is a social activity.*

That was depressing, and so self-indulgent. "You're free!" he told himself. "So what are you whinging about?"

I'm in solitary confinement.

HE WAS JUST BEGINNING to think life all too much of a bother when Mrs Ma became a bother.

She was a bit of a fish out of neighbourhood. She would have been lost in the crowd of grandmother types in the Haymarket's Chinatown, with their black cotton slippers and comfortable, dumpy, quilted cotton jackets, but here she was alone. She'd come just after opening, standing on the pavement in front of his shop, holding up a bouquet of two lilies to sell, or a bunch of three garlic bulbs; always some little thing.

She was selling them, and yet not, her technique being that she would look away when someone took pity on her and was going to buy out of charity. One day after unsuccessfully not managing to repel, she sold her bouquet of two camellias desperately in need of botox.

She entered his shop, bought two oranges, and positioned herself on the pavement again, in her usual place, right in front of his shop, her two oranges held out for sale.

He invited her in, opened a folding chair, and made tea.

He was so unused to talking to anyone, he wouldn't have been able to open her up. But he didn't need to. Mrs Ma's family lived nearby, she said, but they were wanting to move considerably up-neighbourhood, preferably to a unit overlooking the Harbour Bridge. She'd been in Australia two years, brought over from Hong Kong by her banker son, whose wife was also into some sort of finance. She snorted.

"Why did you come?" he wanted to ask but that was way too personal.

"You might ask 'Why did I come?'" she said, wagging her cup for more. "Good question." She hadn't wanted to move any more than her many widowed neighbours had, she said. But Hong Kong could not afford to let a street like hers stay unimproved, not with the price of land underpinning the economy. Oh, she knew a bit about finance, too. So her tight little community had to be 'resettled'. She screwed up her nose at that word. "We were popped out like rice grains in a frying pan."

"My son Richard is a good man. His wife, she's English you know. They don't even want children. I am a burden. I wish he had no pride."

Mrs Ma was a human canary. She just loved talking. Not that she wouldn't listen. She craved communication.

And she warmed him up.

It was an unexpected pleasure hearing her voice, sometimes an exotic puzzle when she used words and idioms he'd never come across., When she really got going, she spoke an archaic Shanghai dialect with tones such as he heard only once: a rare recording of crossover jazz at the Peace Hotel in the racy 20s.

When he mentioned this, she said, "No coincidence. That was me."

She had to be wrong, of course. Little bits she let out about her history were similarly impossible because she couldn't have been born yet. As to the horrors she must have seen, the terrors she'd survived—he could only imagine. She avoided them.

AND THAT WAS JUST the first day. She wormed herself in so much, he must have let on about his garden plot, though she still didn't know about his secret back room.

She begged to see that garden plot. It was worse to keep her away and hurt her feelings than to risk her seeing. He rearranged his dawn schedule of going to the wholesale market and then the plot before the shop opened, to loop around and pick her up in front of the shop at 7 am.

As soon as he lifted her out and down from the truck, all four-foot-something of her, she was uncontrollable, waving him away. It was only moments before she zeroed in on the place he'd most hoped to shield.

She crouched on her heels before the cabbage. It was totally unmarketable, giant untrimmed leaves spreading further than she could spread her arms, each leaf as intricately holed and scalloped as if this were a fan—a fan for an empress. This masterpiece was being worked on by a team too many to be numbered, as Mrs Ma watched, to Arthur Zhang's red-faced shame.

She picked out a cabbage caterpillar and held it up, dangling from her fingers. The way the sun went through it, there was no avoiding the pest.

"Look," she said. "A green lantern!"

She revelled in this garden that she compared to Emperor Taizong's almost mythic private garden of, if she remembered correctly, a thousand years ago or so. "I can't remember exactly when. But," she poked him in the chest, "yours is *much* more beautiful. Certainly more rarefied."

She had a special interest in the gorgeous green cabbage caterpillars, which would have made him think, "This is meant to be" if he gave in to irrational impulses.

But he did tell her about the cabbage caterpillar he and his father had cared for so many years ago.

She didn't say one word during his story. As he heard himself tell it, he felt his face redden. The project was incredibly pointless, effete, stupid.

When he finished, he felt that he had broken something by bringing up a piece of his past so fragile—his mother and father and that little being tied up in its tender bundle—that by taking it out of its shelter of memory, he'd held it out under the harsh rays of exposure, and burnt it.

He had to change the subject, but subtly. "A shame that a caterpillar must become a butterfly."

"No shame," she said quietly, without a trace of her vivacious birdlike voice. "No must."

This was a side of Mrs Ma that had been in the dark. She turned to him full on.

"Why not stay as a caterpillar, waking to eat each day? Now let me dig for a while."

SHE LOVED TO GET down on her knees on a kneeling pad of newspapers. In her quilted brown jacket, she looked like some baby dragon who wanted to be a dog, throwing up soil, huffing into the holes, picking up sticks. She didn't know the first thing about gardening, but that was no inhibition. Nor was she delicate about her interest in the garden shed he'd once lived in. On her second visit to the garden, she had him unlock it for her straight away, then ordered him in. "Your apartment above the shop is a sad place." (He'd never invited her up there, not just because it was depressing, but because of the stairs.)

"Why live there," she said, "when you can live here? You wake up, come here every morning. You could wake up, go there every morning. If I lived here too, I could keep it clean. Make it happy. Cook for you."

She said all this in her most vivacious voice, as if it were a joke. He couldn't respond in any way but laughing in appreciation.

The rest of the visit was tainted with sadness. He hoped she could see his heartache.

The next week had a long weekend. On the holiday Monday she knocked on his shop's roller door earlier than they'd arranged, and he took her to the plot as she asked him to. She'd brought a packet of moon cakes and another of gunpowder tea, for mid-morning. He took the tea but had something else in mind to eat—'a little something I've prepared'.

The only other person he'd cooked for had been his father, who'd only wanted the same most basic, spare and poor food the three of them had shared on the collective farm—quite a contrast to the banquets he took his son to in Beijing.

Spending long hours eating, drinking, and singing at elaborate Party banquets was one of the manifestations of Zhang Chen's restoration as a valued Party member. He took his son to sit at his side, saying the boy helped him hear. After their first joint five-hour session, Zhang Chen apologized to his son. Wenge said he was willing to sacrifice anything for his father, but he never revealed the perverse thrill he got from seeing the soft belly of the Party so exposed.

Hidden in the back rooms of banquet halls, there had to be work units painting scales on scaled fish, constructing full-scale scenes of heroes made of tinted rice. Not everything at the banquets was that sort of thing, though that was always central to the themes. The serious centre of every banquet was eating and drinking, and a banquet, to be considered to have achieved, had to last for as many hours as a successful criticism session.

The only really difficult part of a Party banquet was learning the sleight of hand, the acting necessary in pretending to be drunk. They made quite a picture, father and son, their voices raised high as their glasses at the drunken Party singalongs.

Mrs Ma deserved good taste, not a display of Party hypocrisy. A delicious, intensely comforting feast, best shared in true camaraderie, And what can compare with congee?

He laid it on his rickety garden table.

Instead of the usual plethora of toppings for the plain rice porridge that is congee, he'd laid out just a few homemades. Cubes of sweet-salt turnip pickles, peppery nasturtium buds, fluffy pea-sized inflorescences from native wattle that tasted of camphor and honey and looked like newborn chicks. Instead of the usual grey preserved eggs, he'd dropped raw quail eggs into boiling oil—small suns with liquid cores. A few choice leaves.

She examined everything in minute detail. They ate the proper way, without talking. Her progress was glacial.

SHE CRITICIZED EVERYTHING.

"Grey! You know congee? This is grey. Who taught you how to make congee?"

"I taught myself."

"Imagine if you'd been taught properly. A bowl of white congee." She shuddered. "Like a bowl of boiled lightly crushed false teeth. Only a master knows congee should be just *this*—pearl grey—its texture: silk. It's so perfect, I hate to spoil it with, hmm. . . "

And it went on like this with everything he'd laid out. His heart felt like a fish flopping in a dry bucket, it was going through so much.

Her eyes sparkled with joy, but also something else.

"I would say I was proud of you," she said, "but I can take no credit."

He had to avert his head. He refilled the pot, thinking how precious a grandmother can be. By the time he was composed enough to look at her, a tear was rolling down her face. She wiped it away angrily. "Sinh-de-lah," she said. "I'm like Sinh-de-lah. I wish I could stay. Must get back home before I turn into a pumpkin."

Cinderella! He was surprised she knew that story. He'd only recently learned it as part of his self-education about Western culture. Cinderella must have been turned into a Hong Kong girl who needed to be rescued.

There was no delicate way to say what he had to. "Do they beat you?"

"Of course not! But I have no life with them. And they have no life." She leaned forward as if she was worried someone else might hear. "They're so *boring*."

SHE LOVED TO BRING him gifts, bought with the little pocket money her son gave her.

She was a terrible nag, not letting up on Arthur to keep applying for positions he deserved. She was relentlessly supportive of everything but his despair. When he investigated getting into tutoring and found that students didn't want to learn, they just wanted ghost-writers for their work, she shared his disgust.

When she was around, he could almost forget how lonely he was, how purposeless. That Mrs Ma was the only woman in his life and that he got so much out of her made him wonder what his life would be without her. It had only been months, but it seemed like years. One morning he woke with a sore throat. As soon as she arrived, he told her to leave, that he was dangerous. She made a scene, she was so indignant.

The next day the sore throat turned into a wracking cough. He couldn't be near customers.

He was also desperately worried about Mrs Ma. She was who knows how old. He put on a face mask, told her to keep away from him, and that he'd have to close the shop. She argued to keep it open. "I can run it," she said. Preposterous, but *What the hell*, he thought. *She's too strong for me to argue with.* He settled himself for the day in a bedroll amongst the unpacked boxes where he could hear what was going on but not infect anyone.

The customers not only happily greeted her, but thanked her for taking care of that nice man. As for her communication, she uncorked a little something she must have been saving for the occasion— bubbling light crisp English with the same inability to pronounce *r*s as the uppercrust English. She was a hit.

She couldn't wait to come the next day.

By the time she arrived just before opening he'd done his usual dawn run to the wholesale markets, but he'd been too sick to go to the garden.

She hadn't just pitched up. She had dressed up. A quilted silk jacket in cabbage-caterpillar green. The gorgeous butterfly brooch perched on her shoulder was a jeweller's masterpiece, it looked so alive.

Out of a curious silk purse that had seen many better days, she pulled a packet that looked quite as old, its soft wrapper yellowed as a smoker's wall. This had to be some real-deal Chinese herbalist stuff. He remembered his father's words: *Being told a dirty root or a misbegotten penis is good for you negates the Party's responsibility to further scientific health care.*

"Don't turn up your nose at this, boy."

Of course he let her dose him. The taste was horribly bitter, like aspirin.

"Extra-special *lingzhi*," she said, but he obviously knew nothing. "Mushroom of immortality."

He couldn't help grinning. "So it will make me immortal?"

"Of course not, silly! Nothing can stop that. But it will lengthen this stage."

THE NEXT MORNING HE woke feeling, actually, *terrific*. That was definitely the word, in English. He was almost disappointed for Mrs Ma. She'd so loved nursing him.

He felt so good that he'd made her a fragrant bouquet of geranium leaves, each deep green leaf exquisitely mined till the tunnels glowed palest celadon. He put it in a glass of water in his secret back room, the 'buggy room' where he stored his picks from his own plot for the special few of his customers, those who have true taste, who appreciate the truly organic.

As soon as he opened the roller door, he was run off his feet. He'd never had a day like this. People must have been waiting for him to open, like they stand around the doors of banks. Many customers smiled at him for no reason. Several asked if he was feeling better. They seemed to genuinely *want* him to be well. One actually asked, "Where's that nice lady, your grandmother?"

He felt, for the first time, that Zhang's Infinite Immortals Fruit and Veg wasn't just a shop, but a little village such as only occurs in Western fiction, where people care about each other and visit with plates of cakes.

At 10 am, one did. Melmet Bulgurluoğlu from next door came bearing a plate smelling of sunwarmed orange-flowers and honey, a horrifying sight.

"Mrs Bulgurluoğlu! I'm so sorry! I have no excuse."

"From little birds that tell me, you have many," she smiled. "But you're busy. If you have our order—"

"Of course I do! Here, I'll wheel it over now."

"But you have so many customers!"

"Go, Mr Zhang," said a woman whose visits always made him uncomfortable because he didn't want to be caught staring. She was a Persian miniature come to life, her nose as fanciful as any dragon, and every bit as gorgeous. She waved him away gaily, saying "Leave us so we can pinch the tomatoes behind your back."

He went out back and stacked a trolley high with a selection he'd bought that dawn especially for the Bulgurluoğlus, as he did and had done, six days a week, almost as long as he'd had the shop. It was all so second-nature as part of his life by now that forgetting to deliver this morning shocked him with its unnaturalness, like forgetting to breathe. He'd even shopped for them and delivered at the normal time during the last few days when he'd been so sick, he didn't touch their produce without plastic gloves. That his excuse for forgetting to deliver today was that he was happy was the poorest excuse of all. But where *was* Mrs Ma?

In the meantime, Melmet Bulgurluoğlu unveiled her plate, and to the great relief of the tomatoes, the flock of customers' fingers descended on the warm sticky *tulumba tatlisi*, and soon half a dozen mouths were eating and uttering at the same time—half-incoherent murmurs of delight and praise, pleasing but frustrating to Mrs Bulgurluoğlu. "Take another. Another," she urged. "Empty the plate." And soon enough, they dropped what she'd been waiting for—many delicious titbits for her hungry ears.

When Arthur returned, she hadn't left, so he didn't know what to do with himself. He couldn't count the years since they had spoken. She was lovely as ever, almost overripe. He'd never noticed how sad her eyes looked. He couldn't ask her anything in front of these customers, but he felt a pang of guilt for not trying to help these wonderful people all these years.

"Arthur," she said. "You were so slow. Don't you like my cooking?"

"Me? How? You're the best cook in the *world*."

"Wash your mouth," said the Persian miniature. "Your mother's memory."

"He's a good boy, Fazlur," said Melmet. "His mother was a professor. In bad times."

"Shame upon me, Mr Zhang! I should have known."

"I don't know if this is the right thing to say," said Arthur. "Estağfurullah."

"'Estağfurullah' is always right," smiled Melmet.

"All *right*, we're finished here," she said to a woman who had nothing in her hands but had just said "Excuse *me!*" like ice dropped on your head.

THE WOMAN WAITED POINTEDLY. She was dressed expensively and her watch was thin as the most overpriced wafer chocolate. She looked as interested in fruits and vegetables as a computer's hard-drive.

"Please shut the shop," she said. "I hope you know I had to take the day off."

"And you are?"

"I told you. Close the shop."

"Excuse *me*. If you are concerned about customers hearing you, please don't worry. They have left, so what is your problem, please?" She couldn't see them, but he could, what looked like the whole bunch hanging around on the pavement. He pitied them having only human ears.

"Right," she said, her pursed lips rayed like the flag of the rising sun. "You want to play hardball."

"Please. I'm at work." He barely swallowed *What's your game?* A customer came in. A *special* customer. "Mrs Jordan," he said. "The *bami* you wanted. Would you mind looking after things while I get it?"

Mrs Jordan was sharp. She nodded and strolled over to just short of the bitch's comfort space. Arthur took a while in his secret room, though it would have only taken a moment to grab the basket of the lovely, slightly lacy okra he had picked that morning for Norma Jordan. He hadn't been this riled for years. He needed to call upon all his experience of being needled, bullied, intimidated.

But first he had to stop shaking. . .

He dealt with Norma Jordan efficiently, thanking her with his eyes.

Ms Rising Sun was in his face again.

"If you don't close the shop," she said, "I'll call the police."

"Madam," he said, and was pleased to see how much she hated that. As one customer explained to him early on, *If you call a woman 'Madam' you can't be faulted technically, because it's polite service, but she will be hurt and therefore angry at you because it means you regard her as old.*

"Madam," Zhang repeated. "This is a business. Please state your business. I'm sure we can clear up your problem in no time." He made himself stretch his lips into an obsequious smile.

His hands were slick with sweat. He felt helpless as when he saw 'customers' stealing for the sake of it. Just last week a kid picked out a beautiful fat head of broccoli as he watched, and ran off with it, laughing his head off. What made Arthur the saddest at his own impotence was that the brat made sure Arthur saw him toss it into the busy road to be instantly splatted. "So bad children," said the sole customer, a woman who, like Arthur, felt heart flutters at the thought of *police*.

The woman in his face waved her hands in a *get lost* sign to two customers who drifted in.

"Don't disturb yourself, Mr Zhang," said the Persian miniature. "We just need to look and think. My daughter's wedding, you know."

"No problem, Mrs Boaz," he said. "Take your time. There's paper and a pen by the till. Here. And do try these kumquats."

"Now," he said to Rising Sun. "Let's just stand over here by the potatoes, so we're not quite as much in everyone's way. You were saying?"

"Very well," she said, "If you don't mind your dirty laundry being washed in public, what have you done with her?"

"With whom?"

"My mother-in-law, of course. If it weren't for Richard, I'd have slapped you with a restraining order so fast your head would spin."

Arthur Zhang's head *was* spinning. This couldn't be, but had to be. "Mrs Ma? Are you Mrs Ma?"

"She is. Don't play dumb."

"That lovely old woman!" "I thought she was his grandmother."—whispers loud as crisps being eaten by someone trying to be quiet in a library.

"That lovely old woman," her daughter-in-law shot back. "*You* should be cursed with her."

The story came out like home-brewed beer exploding. Richard had imported his mother a year ago, saying the old woman wouldn't be a bother. That she'd be so out of her depth here, she'd only come out of her room to clean and cook for them. That he had to do his duty to her, but she wouldn't last long. "Richard said six months max. We need to move to the flat we're having built for us. We certainly can't have her in *that* neighbourhood, and can you imagine us trying to entertain our contacts?

"She's a nightmare. She disappears every day. Richard insists she doesn't have Alzheimer's but what would he know? She needs to be put in a home, hardly something we can afford. My husband has this ridiculous Chinese sense, no offence, of filial honour. But what does she know of that? I had to hire a detective behind his back, but she told us last night anyway. Imagine Richard's shame when she called you her grandson and told us she was moving into your market garden shed. That was it. I'd already arranged because Richard is such an avoider. Today I was going to take the day off to get her settled in her new home, with her own kind. There's excellent security. And now she's gone. And Richard doesn't know. And I've had the detective comb through your plot and your shed, and he says she isn't there. He's also gone through your shop from the back, so you mustn't have her here. I can't bear to see that shed, and I don't know how Richard would be able to take seeing it, or her. Are you even *listening?*"

Zhang picked up his head and looked her in the eyes.

She touched her nose with a tissue. "You should be charged."

The two women clutched each other. Another from the crowd was now absentmindedly gorging on grapes.

"How could she want to live with *you*?" Mrs Ma's daughter-in-law asked. "In your garden shed!"

"Where *is* Mrs Ma?" he asked, very quietly and calmly. He'd never been more frightened in his life. He'd never known where she actually lived, how she got to his shop, nor how she got home. She had said something about needing to disappear "like Sin-de-lah" and he'd respected that.

"You don't know?"

"How I wish I did!" His voice broke. "I should have taken better care of her." He hid his face in his hands, his shoulders shaking uncontrollably.

"Lady," said a familiar voice, someone who had shopped here from the first week but who had always been just as shy as Zhang. "I would be most careful if I were you."

"And who the hell are you?"

"Shut up already. We've already witnessed: public nuisance, harassment, obstructing a business. And you've charged yourself with a slew of others:

accessory to B and E, bad enough but nothing compared to section 348 of the Criminal Codes Act. Abuse of a senior, a fine lady we could bear character witness to also." She took out a notebook and pen. "Actually, let's not beat around the bush. Please state your full name and address."

Mrs Ma's daughter-in-law was so red-faced that "Don't pop a gasket" laughed someone. "Get out," said another.

"Let's be specific," said a plump middle-aged woman in a persimmon and lime sari. "Scuttle out!"

To the audience's delight, they saw a human scuttle—and even better, the scuttler was heard loudly arguing with a traffic warden, and then a cop.

"Thank you. All of you," said Arthur.

"She was lying about the investigator," said Kavitha Gopalan. "She's spent nothing."

"How can you tell?"

She touched her nose. "And please warn me the next time you play lawyer, Zahir. I almost giggled. I'll never again be too snobby to watch crime shows."

"Ladies," said the woman in the sari. "I missed you at class. Now don't lie to me. The idea is—first muscles, then mouths. Exercise class, and *then* Ali

Baba's. Not Ali Baba's instead. Come on. I'll fit you in a session now."

"But Priya—"

"No buts."

Her flock emptied the shop but for one grizzled Croatian man who'd stood unnoticed the whole time.

"That nice ol lady. She okay," he said. "She hiding from bad children. She do escape."

"Thank you," said Arthur. "There's always hope." He'd always hated that facile truism, but said it because he'd thought it was expected. From the Croatian's startled expression, he knew how gruesomely wrong he was.

That night Mrs Ma's butterfly brooch came to him in a dream—flying in, pinless, through the open window. It landed on his open palm and closed its wings in repose. *Such a comforting sign* Melmet would say. But she read Turkish coffee mud.

MELMET COULDN'T HAVE BEEN happier. She had been looking for an opportunity to break this crazy and terrible shyness that had come over them all like some witch's curse.

"Go to him," she told Bülent.

He shook his shaggy, silver-streaked head. His eyes were so tragic, he looked funny. "I'm just a big clumsy bear. I know I'll fail."

"You know nothing about yourself."

He'd see. He was joy itself, given the chance. *Okay, a jolly bear.* They needed each other. *Maşallah! We all need Arthur and he needs us.*

MELMET WAS RIGHT YET again. The connection between Arthur and the Bulgurluoğlus was joyfully and gratefully repaired, stronger than ever. Arthur was also gratified to know he actually gave some pleasure to his customers.

But it was, come every nighttime, another night alone, another little step in the trudge of years passing with no reason to trudge with them.

He began looking for movement in the stone he still had left from his father. All was still.

Sleep. Sleeplessness. Memories. Waking dreams. Dreaming wakes.

"Turn off that racket."

He was in bed with his eyes closed, trying to sleep out two earworms—a particularly ironic song from his collective farm days that had mated with that other obnoxious hit, "I still call Australia home". They stopped with what sounded like a loudspeaker being smashed.

"What are you making of yourself?" He was surprised. In the darkness on silent nights, he'd heard voices many times, but he could never make out words. He'd read up on the condition and chalked it up to the state of emptiness. Being alone made your brain compensate, just not enough to be believable. Maddening—to hear as if you are eavesdropping, *but you can never make out what they're saying.*

This voice, however, was not only clear, but it was his mother, talking just as she had. He'd almost forgotten the clarity of her diction, the loveliness of her tones.

"Enough laying around," said his father.

He sat up in bed. Rubbing his eyes free of the dream, he turned on the light to make himself a cup of tea.

And there they were before him—his father and his mother, sort of floating and semi-solid. Arthur wouldn't have known his mother, but for her voice.

She looked younger than he'd ever seen her, and pretty. His father was as he remembered: the desiccated praying mantis with homemade spectacles.

"Where's Yoda?" he said. "I'm goddamn done for."

He left the room and made himself the tea, but they didn't go. Instead, they firmed up till they were as solid as cheese.

At first he was truly goddamned terrified that he'd lost it. That the only thing he could do was to hang himself. But he couldn't do that to the Bulgurluoğlus. So he heard them out.

When his father met his mother again after he had died, he had a change of heart about her grasp on reality. "It's a shame it took that long," he said to Arthur. "Your mother should have tried harder to convince me when I was alive."

"And have you lose your job?" she snorted. "Remember when we had to eat?" She pointed to Arthur. "He still does."

"You have your grandfather's hairs, boy," she said. "We were waiting for the fourth to drop."

"Boy?" Arthur made a sound that could have been laughter. "Do you know how old I am?"

"Fifty-two today," said his father. "What are you doing with it?"

"Time is running around you and you're doing nothing with it," said his mother. "Reality is that song that isn't there. But it *is* there. Those thoughts you have about butterflies and caterpillars and what-ifs. Yes, we know about them."

"Perpetual Infinity, my arse," she added, ever the linguist. "Time is everything and nothing."

"Truly see it," his father said. "Reality. And—"

"Fuck around with it."

They left Arthur with a commitment to do something he'd mulled over for years—something completely ridiculous, irrational, unbelievable. Something the scientist part of his brain recoiled from. Something now irresistible. . .

He'd still have thought resistance the only way. But his father's present airy-fairyness yet undeniable realness destroyed critical cells in his cerebral cortex.

But what made him most certain that this was all real was this:

His dead mother was still picking up languages.

THE SELECTION HAD BEEN planned meticulously by Arthur Zhang. Bülent Bulgurluoğlu was no help in the science but a wonderful partner, his enthusiasm smothering Arthur Zhang's self-doubts.

The mating had been thought out in detail, too. The little Cabbage White was one of a cloud of them released just after his 'escape' at 11 am. In his case, release wasn't really accurate. He was so content in his cell that Arthur had to carefully net him and toss him out of the premises.

Arthur had thought the meeting and mating between him and the Painted Lady would take place in moments, at which time she would naturally come home to the security and comfort of her cell. So when he lost sight of her, he was most distraught till Bülent barrelled out of Ali Baba's and shoved Arthur out to see, tossing back to him—"Go to the kitchen. I'll watch the store."

And there she was, perched on a ruby pomegranate seed in the middle of an ocean-sized bowl of something that looked to Arthur Zhang like a recipe stolen from the Chinese. That creaminess, that silken sheen. The Painted Lady was sucking up the rose-scented stuff as if she'd been born to drink only this. She had an audience—or was it a line-up of servants?

"Why haven't I seen that before?" whispered Arthur. "That's our congee, just with different ingredients."

"People won't eat grey stuff," said Sami. "This is just for our family."

"They *should*," hissed Melmet. "We only make it for special times. It's *aşure*—Noah's Ark pudding."

Just when the butterfly looked as if she were pausing to drink more, she flew out of the kitchen. And thus began her sampling.

Arthur tore himself away to go back to work.

Mr Bulgurluoğlu was a big clumsy bear in the kitchen, Melmet always said, and the children could run the restaurant without him, so they had told him to take the day off. He kept out of the Painted Lady's way, but ran next door every few minutes to give Arthur reports. By the time the hookahs came out, they were both watching together.

No one had taken in consideration the dangers to butterflies of second-hand smoke. Who would think the creature would get near? When she did, Bülent Bulgurluoğlu felt his stomach knot at his thoughtlessness. He expected her to plummet like a bent paper airplane, not begin to roll and... indescribable. At one point he turned to Arthur and whispered, "She should teach belly dance."

After seeing off the disrupters of the mating dance, Bülent Bulgurluoğlu rushed back. Arthur was waiting for him. "She's sleeping," he said. They tiptoed to the entrance of that most important, secret back room, the only space she'd ever known till the door opened for her that morning. That she'd returned was— Arthur was ashamed to be infected by modern culture with the thought—*nothing short of a miracle*. His scientific mind spat angrily, reminding him that her retreating back to her cell was her only possible voluntary response. She knew nothing else. *Her cell is her security.*

THE NEXT MORNING, BÜLENT took the dawn watch. Arthur couldn't. He had to be at Flemington Markets at 4:30 to get the best buys. Then he had to stop at the garden to harvest his exclusives. Arthur's love and enthusiasm stretched far enough that he half-hoped Bülent saw the Laying. But his humanity stole the other half. Although he expected a dawn to be her

Time, he did wish she'd stay up late again, very late, so she would do it before the both of them at midnight when Bülent put Ali Baba to sleep and he came over for their nightly tea and chat.

The day passed strangely. Both men could do almost nothing useful, they were so anxious and excited. Yet she did nothing. Oddly nothing. She slept.

Day after day, no matter whose watch, she seemed to be in a torpor. She supped languidly but didn't lay.

ONE 9 AM, MR ZHANG bustled in late cursing to himself about the tomatoes from the wholesale market that had stunk so much of pesticide, he'd had to run upstairs to shower and change his clothes before entering the sanctum. Bülent was used to these grumbles, but he greeted his friend with fear for him, and sadness. "I think she's sick, Arthur. She's going back and forth, on everything, flaps her wings, and leaves."

Indeed, she seemed different. She looked drunk there, perched on the lavender flower.

But Arthur knew better.

She dropped, catching a wing, which tore apart as she fell the rest of the way to the potting soil.

Bülent's eyes prickled as tears sprang from them. She would never fly again.

Her legs cycled a few times, moving her in a partial circle. She half-opened a wing and shut it, open and closed. Bülent's moustache began to shine, and with great difficulty, he caught an audible sob.

But Arthur didn't seem disturbed, hardly at all. He was crying, too, silently, but he was also almost smiling.

"Arthur. Arthur!" *Of course!* Bülent said to himself. *In Arthur's panic to get down here and cleaned up, he forgot to put his hearing aid back in.* Without it, Arthur was deaf as a cabbage.

The butterfly flipped herself over to the other side, which made Bülent want to howl.

"The Painted Lady is dead," he mumbled.

"Not necessarily, Bülent," said Arthur.

"You heard me?"

"Of course. A line is just something unfinished for it has an end. 'Glorious' is a poisoned clot dumped upon a line to stunt its growth."

"I never knew you to be so... poetic?"

Arthur chuckled. "You can be so diplomatic. I was just remembering something my mother taught me, and told me never to say out loud. People on a collective farm weren't diplomatic. The thing continues. 'Wipe away the clot and the line can grow—and every line that can grow all the way, grows into a circle that never ends.'"

He shrugged. "That circle of life thing sounds so New Age, so unscientific. She'd never have wanted my father to know she taught me this."

Bülent could hardly believe that his friend, who'd been obsessed for months, was talking such... such *waffle*.

And Arthur was looking everywhere but at the elephant in the room.

Bülent got up, gesturing toward a crowded little table in the corner. "Melmet came in a while ago. Seeing you were late, she thought you'd like a nibble."

On the table were two plates of baklava.

Arthur rushed over and picked up both plates, holding them close to his chest. Then he, with reluctance, held one out, pulling back when his friend's hand touched it. He kicked away a pile of newspapers on the floor and laid the two plates down.

"Put on your reading glasses, and kneel, Bülent. Kneel and look at this plate."

Bülent was insulted. His wife Melmet not only made the best baklava in Australia. They *never* bought in pastries, as other restaurants did! But she was such a fanatic about cleanliness that he was always more comfortable in this little room, with his soil-under-the-fingernails-friend.

"Bülent, think!" Arthur exclaimed, practically dancing in place. "Get down. Put on your specs. Don't touch it. Remember. The size of a pinhead."

The penny dropped in Bülent's brain.

They looked and looked, and with the white plates and the strange glare of the gro-lights or no artificial lights at all, all they could see was the grated emerald piles of pistachio, the glowing cream and gold strata layers of pastry and nuts, and the shiny honey-syrup—nectar of the gods, covering the mountains and flowing out on the glazed white stoneware.

They looked till they had to keep rubbing their eyes to focus, till their shoulders and knees screamed abuse.

Finally, Arthur pushed himself up. "I'm sorry. I just hoped—"

"My aunt's moustache!"

And it's true. Bülent's ejaculation was an understatement.

In the shadowed upturn, safe from being drowned was one (1) egg.

Arthur had always loved beautiful things, as had his parents. To his mother, it was language and words and sentiments and an irrational strain of something dangerous resembling optimism. Arthur's grandfather had known jade, fine ceramics, knew all the nuances of delicate green celadon ceramic glazes But all those—gems and glazes, rocks and clays—the commonest cabbage butterfly caterpillar could put all of that to shame. The finest padded velvet—caterpillar green—decorated with sulphur and pitch.

The emeralds on the wing of a butterfly could, unlike anything Grandfather saw, change to topaz/ruby/sapphire silken black.

But a butterfly's egg was carved far more delicately and with more grace than any fortune-dripping jade treasure. And if the world could have a perfect gem, it would be a cross between the eggs of a Painted Lady and that of a Cabbage White. Celadon green, more translucent than the finest porcelain, the shape: the shape—too perfect to be made by any master, these vases remind one of the melon shapes so favoured once hundreds of years ago, but this had been taken to an impossibly refined degree, with hundreds of the finest hooks bristling from ridges running its length— the whole too small to see without a glass.

"But for your wife," said Arthur.

"She must have been in such pain."

"Your wife?"

"Her!"

"Yes, of course."

ARTHUR HAD RESEARCHED EVERYTHING, hoping for the best. He knew that his father's early work had been based on the flawed work of Lysenko, so he twiddled it to change the theory from that of 'if plants are crowded together close enough, the urge to compete will be driven out of them and all will thrive' to 'if animals are deprived of each other enough, the urge to mate will drive them to thrive on anyone, regardless of who it is'.

Thus his theory arranged the marriage of naiveté and desperation between the Painted Lady and the Cabbage White.

That it had succeeded he celebrated in his quiet, unbombastic way. Now, however, he had to make the next stage count. In his unending reading, he had come upon the legend of the immortality mushroom. His mother had talked about it a few times, but only when they were alone. He knew even as a five-year-old, how his father would take this 'teaching', so he kept this rubbish she believed in to himself, and never laughed at her credulity. After all, he thought. I thought there was an old woman with a broom in the moon till I was three. Some people never grow out of some ridiculous delusions.

But since she'd been proven right about ghosts, he thought to give it a shot.

As soon as the butterfly egg hatched into a grub, he fed it a butterfly-grub portion of the same mushroom of immortality brew that Mrs Ma had given him and made him take so long ago, for it had certainly made him feel good when he took it, and he had never dosed himself with it, so he still had the large parcel of it. The grub resisted, so he took it too, and then the grub took its dose willingly. The stuff was vile-tasting, so it was a special moment every morning when he and his little charge took their tonic.

The grub was properly, a caterpillar, but that word seemed way too grand for the thing that had a head sporting long black bristles, and a body as mottled as a breeding sow.

No matter. To its servants, it was as rubies, and was proffered up all the specialities of Ali Baba's that it could want, many of which Melmet invented specially for the creature—dishes that surpassed anything Arthur had ever seen for humans.

In a month, the grub lost its bristles and started changing its look. By six months old, it was rather beautiful. Bright cabbage-caterpillar green, velvety, with two large, meltingly gorgeous, ever-vigilant false eyes near its bottom.

When it would naturally have spun its silk cocoon to pupate till it emerged as a butterfly, it continued to eat, moulted again and grew, moulted again and grew.

Sami took it upon himself to create even more toothsome temptations, such as his divinely sweet and chewy grape and walnut *cevizli sucuk* sticks that took three weeks of dipping and a month of curing, which the caterpillar loved so much and was so greedy about, it looked at times like the Hindu goddess Kali, wielding sticks in a halo of 'hands'.

At each moult, it emerged more beautiful, more regal or goddessish till no one could call it *it*, but the titles suggested didn't fit.

Empress. Sultana. Queen. All those titles were common, compared to her.

Mondays, Ali Baba's was closed, so on Monday nights her whole Court would shove themselves into the space behind the fruit shop to boggle, gaze, and frankly, stare in awe. Hurrem and Sami were possibly the most astounded, for what young people are interested in the stuff their parents watch? They had thought, only a year before, that the caterpillar thing and its secrecy some silly babysitting exercise to help their lonely 'uncle' Arthur. That was before the caterpillar's third or so moult.

Now she was as tall as Sami, as thick as his father, and so beautiful was her natural coat that it was almost a shame to have to clothe and pad her, but she was as sensitive as any unelected ruler.

Tonight they simply had to give her a title. 'Her' and 'she' and 'the great one' had gone on for too long. She had just unveiled her latest look, her skin still wet with that delicate glow of tenderness. With each shedding of the old, a new pattern was revealed. This was the most magnificent yet. It had a beauty that struck Bülent so violently that his eyes streamed tears.

She was ineffably beautiful, but she also reminded him of something, something he couldn't remember.

"Idiot!" Sami burst out. He struck his hand to his forehead and ran out the back. They could hear him opening the back door to Ali Baba's, and a couple minutes later he returned carrying a pile of papers that had been carefully wrapped in a black silk shawl. "These were still upstairs in the trunk."

"Of course," said Bülent. "I was going to frame them. I thought that trunk was lost. Didn't I tell you as a child not to open it?"

"Vay canına!" shouted Melmet. "Show us."

"Do the honours, Dad," said Sami.

Bülent pulled out an exquisite marbled sheet of paper—the exact pattern and coloration as the caterpillar.

"We should call her Ebru," said Sami. "That's our Turkish marbled paper art," he said to Arthur. "And yes, Dad. There's more to me than bodybuilding and food culture."

AT TWO YEARS, EBRU was a sight for a Court. Her presence was a massively inconvenient but nevertheless fanatically kept State secret, only known to the Bulgurluoğlus and Arthur. Dressed in a red silk robe which only Arthur had the skill to make—so many sleeves!—the great Ebru spent her days on a luxuriously padded divan, either munching noisily or enjoying her hookah, her favourite flavour of which was, curiously, Bubble Gum—a great disappointment to the traditionalists, but the taste wants what the taste wants.

Communication was a problem. She loved an audience, and resented being left alone. But just as they deduced she would want the hookah, they had to guess what she wished for at other times, for her utterances were many and constant, but in a language foreign to everyone's ears.

The day she said something they all agreed to mean "I demand to be taken out"—a series of high-pitched squeaks—they almost complied, but couldn't. The Bulgurluoğlus were all for disguising her and taking her to Arthur's garden, but he thought it was too risky with all those high-rises looming over the plot.

Ebru ate in obvious grief, and within a month moulted three more times. She now dwarfed Bülent and needed a new regal seat. The little room had become a battery pen.

The Bulgurluoğlus and Arthur joined their two buildings upstairs and installed an industrial lift—all work done pragmatically, with no possible council approval and much expected baksheesh.

She was installed upstairs in a shuttered room, painted and decorated to the splendour she deserved. Arthur slept on the floor on a mat he rolled up during the day.

She lounged in resplendent robes on a regal divan much more comfortable than a throne, eating and issuing clouds of fragrant hookah smoke, everything looking as if this was all meant to be. Every day started out with the chief servant, Arthur, dispensing with a golden spoon, the tincture of immortality mushroom followed by congee that he kept challenging himself to make ever more irresistible. Trays of *baklava*, *irmik tatlisi*, and *zerde* from Ali Baba were carried up in a steady stream, coating the walls of the room with constant fragrance—saffron, rose, cardamom. But what pricked Arthur's heart with jealousy was the great preference Ebru had for the

Turks' grey takeoff from congee, *aşure*—Noah's Ark pudding. She vastly preferred it to congee. If she could have made herself understood, she would have explained that she didn't like the salt in the toppings on congee, where even the sweet was saddened with salt, whereas *aşure* in all its sweet silken richness was the closest thing to happiness that a pudding can be.

No one could remember when she let it be known she was a reader, but as soon as she did, books aplenty were offered on side tables, and indeed, with all those grasps, Her Greatness could peruse many at the same time. But peevishness increased, and many a book was tossed against the increasingly battered wall. Sometimes out of perverseness, she would pretend to be engrossed in reading, holding the book up to its two beautiful but quite fake eyes.

"Ebru demands to look out the window," she said one day, her body language clear enough that her language-challenged servants understood.

Bülent and Arthur made a finely cut wooden screen and installed it while they fought over whether its inspiration—cut-paper art—was Turkish *kaati* or Chinese *jianzhi*. "Kaati is seven hundred years old," insisted Bülent.

"A child!" scoffed Arthur. "Turkey wasn't a twinkle in the world's eye in the second century, when we were jianzhiing so finely, you'd drown yourself in tears at such beauty."

"You are *so* at cross-purposes," Ebru commented, waving the hookah wand. They were such slow learners, they thought she was talking to herself. Indeed, they had debated for a few years already whether she *could* read or was mesmerized by the patterns on the paper.

Arthur started having nightmares about her wanting to be free. *But caterpillars are never supposed to want freedom, only food.* Weren't they supposed to be in the state of butterfly infancy? In this state, he had planned for her to be content for as long as he lived in his state.

YEARS PASS. SO many years.

So many years that after all that *before*, there have been many an *after* after—and an infinity to drive you nuts, of *later*s.

Millions of ghost-making episodes of time ago, Arthur told Bülent Bulgurluoğlu, "Every line that can grow all the way, grows into a circle that never ends."

And *still*, the ends of the line haven't met. Indeed, their curve might be merely the horizon.

FISHES SWIM THROUGH WINDOWS in Sydney's skyscrapers.

In one instance of *before*, as a present to ease the pain of the compulsory acquisition of every building on the street to fit the state's high-rise plan, Sami and Hurrem had sent their parents on a world cruise. The ship was bombed and sunk with no survivors, the instigator for another named world war. Bülent's ghost is a shadow of his former self, shuffling the world over, looking for his beloved wife. Sami had always scoffed at drug companies' profit-making scams, but nothing short of immortality mushroom could have stopped his heart attack. Hurrem distinguished herself in the medical corps, so much so that her name went on some electronic plaque.

And Ebru?

Ebru grew so large in that upstairs room that one night, Sami, Bülent, and Arthur tore off the roof and ceiling. Ebru, wrapped securely by Hurrem, was lifted by crane and lowered into a wide-bodied shipping crate, and long-hauled out of the city by Sami, who had obtained a trucker's license for this eventuality.

They installed her in a completely unnoteworthy windowless cube of a warehouse with no windows. Inside it was a Palace of Delights. She had at her many elbows, more fine foods than she could ever eat. Arthur had created beautiful gardens full of fruits, flowers, smells. And for the first time in her life, he had opened it up with endless mountainous vistas he had cleverly created with a combination of *trompe l'oeil* painting and two walls of mirrors.

She grew and moulted, grew and moulted.

But she grew more and more fretful, restless, cheepy and sometimes (Arthur hated to admit it) irrationally imperious.

When Hurrem diagnosed the problem, Arthur gritted his teeth. Gratefulness was obvious in both sets of Ebru's eyes—and blame.

Why hadn't I discovered her sickness? he berated himself. Why Hurrem?

His shame didn't end there that day. His own mother dropped in, briskly introduced herself to Hurrem, who to her credit, didn't bat an eye. And they put their heads together and prescribed a new lifestyle.

"Great One," said Arthur's mother to the caterpillar, "All your robes and all your cushions and waterbed cannot keep you from pressure sores. You will wish a death your beloved Arthur has screwed you out of having, if we don't do something about *this*."

The poke she gave Ebru *hurt*, reminding Arthur of how unromantic and unable to stomach authority his mother was.

Soothing medicaments were compounded and applied, and she was automatedly pulled and turned for exercise.

But what made the difference was the new diet imposed by Arthur's mother "for as long as this state lasts".

Food to make Ebru not interested in food. Food to survive on. Arthur's mother's cooking.

Arthur took to opening and clutching to his breast the infinitely precious contents of the trunk that held, from the first tiny fingernail-sized moult to that of an elephant, every skin Ebru had ever shed. She would never grow and shed another.

Arthur went into a decline that might have been mirrored by Ebru, so similar were they.

Ebru was bored to distraction.

Arthur had lost his purpose.

Every night he curled in the corner, ready for service, in the grand tradition of lackeys.

His mother and father was taken up by themselves.

Ebru was an infinitely unhappy prisoner in her golden cage.

Arthur wished he was able to die, and to take Ebru with him to that next state.

One day he told her these morbid thoughts. Her beautiful fake nether eyes stared at him dully. They were now cursed with crows-feet, so much weight had she lost.

He turned away, he was so upset. There was no way out.

Bang bang bang! Someone was at the door! No one's secret code. It was locked, of course. No one could get in.

The handle turned. Obviously, knocking had been just a formality. Arthur leapt up, trembling. "I'll protect you!" he yelled to Ebru.

The door flew open to reveal—

"Mrs Ma!"

So LONG AGO.

Evolved fishes swim through the coral reef that was once Sydney's skyscrapers.

Is Arthur and the mysterious Mrs Ma's relationship now: grandmother and grandson? mother and son? Lovers? This is no kiss and tell. She hasn't aged a day. His face is smooth as teak. His four white chin hairs jut out as proudly as his grandfather's still do. Arthur and Mrs Ma could sing songs of glory about their mutual love and the happiness each has found in the other. Their charge, however, is anything but.

On the cloud-swathed peak of a mountain made into a ghost by geological time well before there was human language, she resides in a new improved Palace of Delights. In the same windowless cube, Arthur has installed even more beautiful gardens; and his clever combination of *trompe l'oeil* painting and two walls of mirrors has been trumped up to breathtaking degree, to now give views that are positively vertiginous.

Immortals tend her and go down from the mountain every so often to gather up her food: post-apocalyptic grub.

She has no pressure sores and has reduced to the size of a 20th century Californian tract house.

Only here could she be assured of peace. The lands of Earth are teeming with the ill-willed, the scheming, the disrespectful. Down there, there is nowhere to hide.

Arthur and Mrs Ma are allowed up here to visit, but not having been born Immortal, they are not allowed to stay.

Mrs Ma is finding it increasingly difficult to enjoy Arthur. He used to be such fun.

So on this visit, she has decided she must be an emissary, a difficult job for one such as she, who Arthur once called *undiplomacy incarnate*.

She just told Ebru her plans, and can tell by the caterpillar's alarmed vibrations and chitterings, that Arthur isn't alone in his assessment. And maybe this is indeed, a rash plan of hers. Who knows what the goddess would decide? Immortals born to their state can be unbearably touchy.

Ebru asks for Arthur to be her champion—to beg if needs be, the mercy of the Goddess.

His heart sings with joy.

They were all hoping, of course, that he could be granted an audience with Guanyin, immortal goddess of love and mercy.

He dispatches himself immediately, and is greeted with "Her Love and Mercifulness is out."

Instead, he is granted an appointment to bend his knee to an Immortal who must have kept to the shadows. Neither he, Mrs Ma, nor Ebru has ever heard of her.

"Great," says Mrs Ma. "You can never tell about those oldie moldies. This one's got a title that fits the times."

ARTHUR BOWS AND TOUCHES his forehead. "Most Supreme One," he says as an opening to the Goddess of the Stages of Life.

"*Please*. Get on with it!" she says, exactly as his mother would. And she wrinkles a nose no Immortal would choose to wear.

"Too right," he says. "Could you put the beautiful, singular, innocent Ebru out of her misery and end this stage of her life, so she can progress on her lifeline? She needs and deserves freedom."

"And?"

"And if you would grant this wish, I promise I will be there for her, as I have been since before she was born, to the end of this stage of my life, which is all I can promise for I am still in the dark about what happens—"

"Succinctly put," says the goddess, who he notices is not inclined to illuminate him on afters.

"You have," she says, "dosed yourself and that poor caterpillar with altogether too much Mushroom of Immortality for me to legally grant shortening this stage of the caterpillar's life to less than another aeon. But you knew not what the consequences were of what you planned, so I will waive the letter of the law and use my discretion to grant Ebru's request."

"When?" Arthur would have blurted, but his diplomat genes choke that off and make him bow deeply before he remembers how it irritates her.

But she doesn't look too pissed off. Her lips are tight at the edges. She's holding back a laugh.

"We thank you," he says. "I will pass on your message."

Immortals take forever to do anything, so he looks forward to the time when he and Mrs Ma will hear from Ebru that she is expecting, feeling some change coming on. With the metabolic speed of glass that she's experienced so far, the change should take an old mortal year or so. It could be such a terrifying time. How long will she pupate? *Will she remember me when she emerges?*

EBRU IS DELIGHTED THAT the goddess has freed her to change, and so excited! She doesn't want to think of the boring stage of wrapping herself up and waiting to emerge. *Don't*, she says to herself, *think of the waiting stage. After that, I'm going to be a butterfly!*

"And then I will meet my match and feel things I've never felt before," Ebru says to Arthur. "And I'll dance in the smoke like my mother." It all comes out as various unintelligible chirps that delight Arthur but would horrify him if he understood.

"I am sorry I told you about that," would have to be his painful reply. "There will only be you."

An ethereal bell rings. He has to leave, not being allowed overnight privileges. It hurts to leave her. He wants to throw his arms around a part of her, but all of her eyes are focused far away.

EBRU'S ONCE-BEAUTIFUL FAKE eyes wink at her reflection. She is writhing. She woke feeling something inside she'd never felt before, something that has made her unusually silent. She is entirely alone, a normal state up here for her, where the Immortals have much better things to do than to tend to whatever is in that large unmarked cube.

Inside her palace, everything is as normal. Gorgeous gardens, inedible food, incredible vistas.

"Adda," she calls.

"Adda. Adda. Adda!" Then she forgets she'd ever made sounds.

Something inside her says this is *it*. The pull is so strong, her whole being is wrapped up in this compulsion.

A contortion wracks her, bending her almost double. She stretches out and repeats—taking her first steps to a wall, for she must get up it to those beams where she will hang herself to wrap herself with silk, and wait.

That wall is too cluttered with greenery. She pulls herself sideways, and some more. The effort is so great, she closes her eyes, and suddenly the wall pushes her at a right angle. She's clinging to the endless vista, dizzy with fear. But instead of falling, the vista is hard. That's curious. She isn't seeing out, but at herself. Aha! Fake skies, like fake eyes. She feels secure again knowing this is not open space, but a wall.

Up she pulls herself. . . and up.

Her third pull-up is too much. The wall tumbles down all over her, covering her with shattered mirrors.

The goddess should have known that Ebru would need a palace re-do, but what do goddesses know of caterpillars?

The floor is slick with Ebru's bright green blood.

Ebru's body glitters from innumerable shards, yet she must bend.

From between her false eyes crinkled in concentration, she pulls a silk filament thick as ship's rope.

AFTERWORD NOTES

BUT FIRST, A WARNING:

While I normally totally never say anything about myself, the following does contain personal stuff.

CABBAGE, MY PICTURE ON the cover and here, is an example of parasitic art, but happily, not one publicly funded. Although I have only taken a photo of the unnamed cabbage growing *en* the unsprayed *plein* air of Edinburgh Botanical Gardens, the picture, if I do say so myself, is art. The beautiful cabbage itself, and the uncredited artists remain anonymous. As to the artists' fine cutwork, it is arguably Turkish *kaati*, Chinese *jianzhi*, or the traditional naïve art of the local Invertebrateans.

IN 1900, CHINESE DIPLOMAT Xu Jingcheng's head became one of the displays at Beijing's Caishikou Execution Grounds. He was executed that year for his perspicacious and bloody brave advice about the costs of breaches to international law. Years later, too late for him to laugh (*unless?*), he was memorialised.

I WOULD HAVE LOVED to talk with the little old man whose show was in that little room in the Military Museum of the Chinese People's Revolution, but there was a minder behind him. I did share a train trip with a Long March veteran and his attendant nurse. He was seeing China, and she was taking most marvelous care of him. At train stops, she rushed out and came back with snacks for him and me. In this year of our anti-internationalism, 2017, also Year of the Rooster, I remember fondly her presents of chicken feet on sticks. Seeing current photos of this popular snack, my first thought was sadness and cheap nostalgia, for now it's processed food. Today, they're clawless.

The nurse and I corresponded till I lost track of her. In her last letter (from one of the many Red Army streets), she wrote, *"Lost many precious time during Cultural Revolution. I am a romantic idealist. I'm just ordinary. I'm just low standard. I'll try my best to do anything. Because I'm trying to find medicine books in English. Not many written in English. I hope you appreciate my passion."*

WHILE IT'S OFTEN THOUGHT that people change their names or bestow names to make someone stand out, I would be willing to bet that the majority of deliberately taken and given names are chosen to blend in, not stand out, to make their bearers if not invisible, then safely 'normal'. The Windsors are one example, but many migrants and people in danger know that names are crucial components of survival tactics. I come from a family whose members on both sides have changed their names so many times, it could be called a tradition. Some had hilarious skill and less perception of others' POV than Buckwheat, the adventurous cow who slipped out of the unsecured gate and hid, peeking out at me from behind a sapling. While not denying their Jewishness, several of my relatives thought that being normal meant you couldn't have a Jewish name. So one uncle changed his to Klein. Another, who wanted to be the all-American man, changed his to Israel Goldstein.

I AM AN IMMIGRANT, having emigrated for political reasons. When I first came to Australia, I was terrified that no one would hire me. Instead, I was working in a finance company within weeks, a kind of place I had never imagined. I'd never worked in a *company* before. I was on a floor where I was the only female, so it came to pass that the men who formerly had made their own tea, expected me to. So I did. They didn't like sassafras tea, so that was that. They made mine without further demur. But they did love to come up to me and say, "Say …. and …..:" just to laugh at my accent.

I'd been hired to be a writer, but I didn't know it was to be a *creative writer*. One of my tasks was to write a report to investors telling them how fortunate they were, management be praised, that they had just lost their shirts. They could have lost their pants.

WE ALL HAVE, OR maybe should have, our private shames. In Beijing almost a year to the day after Tiananmen Square, I asked directions of a middle-aged man in a a sweater no moth would bother with. I don't know why I picked him. Superstitious people would nod. He spoke excellent English, and immediately asked me if we could get a cup of coffee. "I'm a doctor," he said, and then said only about ten words about his life. Suddenly, I felt desperate to get away, so I made some excuse. Then he *begged* me. "You won't have to pay. I'll pay. I won't take much of your time," he said. "I'm sorry," I said, "I have to pack." And I fled.

I barely made it round the corner before bursting into tears. I have never been able to be dry-eyed and cool in the presence of someone in grave danger, who's experienced terrible things and just needs some sympathy, for they know you cannot *really* help. From old people who've been stripped of their animal companions and are now supposed to suck it in nursing 'homes', to this doctor with an epic of a life, goddamn, I'm sorry I can't be with you without making a scene, a dangerous one in the case of a place with too many eyes. I have the highest respect for people who not only help others in the gravest and most dangerous of circumstances, but who do it holding in their own selfish uselessly sympathetic grief.

HÜRREM, NOW. SHE WAS no tea and sympathy, likely to flee puff of stale air. Sulëiman's favourite concubine, this slave pissed powerful people off no end when she built to her specs, in a prime location near the Women's Market, a humungous hospital. And not only that, this place to heal sick people was the real deal. It only made room for a modest mosque with one minaret. She was far more interested in the advancement of science than in hope.

AFTER-AFTERWORD NOTE

IT'S UNSCIENTIFIC TO THINK this anything but coincidence, but after finishing the Afterword notes, I came across the pioneering (under-appreciated) scientific work of Canadian addiction psychologist Bruce K Alexander (see www.brucekalexander.com), who moved lab rats from the standard environment: tiny metal isolation cells in which their only mental escape and possible pleasure was the drug feed literally plugged into them; to a structure he called 'Rat Park', a roomy wooden box where they were no longer alone, had lots of toys, luxurious bedding, and where the rats could look out at verdant vistas on the painted walls.

A Restless Wind by Shahrukh Husain

Zara Hamilton leads an apparently charmed life as a human rights lawyer in London – but she is haunted by questions about her past. Why did her mother disappear? What made her college sweetheart, the Maharaja of Trivikrampur, abandon her? Why did her husband renege on a plan to return to her native India? And why has she avoided visiting her much-loved family home in Qila, Trivikrampur?

After ten years as a Muslim in Britain, bereft of a homeland, Zara finally seeks the answers. When she returns to Qila, her world is shatteringly different, her aristocratic family mired in complications and far-right politics on the rise.

Amid the unrest of a changing nation, Zara seeks the key to her mother's secret as contemporary resentments clash with a harmonious past.

~

The Love Machine & other contraptions by Nir Yaniv

What happens when every wish you make is immediately granted by God? If you could use the power of music to travel through time? If your body was the battleground for a strange, alien invasion?

In this, his debut collection in English, Israeli author Nir Yaniv shows his remarkable versatility, collecting stories from over a decade of writing and a wide range of the fantastic. In turns humorous, lyrical, profound - but always entertaining – these are the haunting tales of an author at the height of his power.

The Iron Wire by Garry Kilworth

In 1870 a young telegrapher travels halfway around the world to help create one of the technological wonders of the Victorian age: the construction of a single galvanised iron wire between Adelaide and Darwin, crossing two thousand miles of wilderness.

The Iron Wire: a novel of human hope and progress in a land where men die, women are widowed, and bushrangers live by the lie and the gun.

~

The Quarantined City by James Everington

The Quarantined City: sealed off from the outside world, with only the sight of the ocean to remind its inhabitants of life beyond. No one knows why the city has been quarantined and conspiracy theories abound.

But for Fellows life continues largely as before. He walks the streets, hunts out rare books; the sun continues to shine and the gulls circle above.

There's the small matter of the ghost haunting his house, but Fellows doesn't let himself think of that.

But when he tracks down a story by the reclusive writer known as Boursier, his old certainties fade as he becomes aware that the secrets of the city, the ghostly child, and the quarantine itself, might be more connected than he thinks...

~

www.infinityplus.co.uk